Also by Rikki Ducornet

The Word "Desire"

The Word "Desire"

RIKKI DUCORNET

An Owl Book

Henry Holt and Company • New York

Henry Holt and Company, Inc.
Publishers since 1866
115 West 18th Street
New York, New York 10011

Henry Holt® is a registered trademark
of Henry Holt and Company, Inc.

Stories in this collection have appeared in *Conjunctions,
Parnassus*, and *The Iowa Review*.

Library of Congress Cataloging-in-Publication Data
Ducornet, Rikki.
The word "desire" / by Rikki Ducornet.
        p.   cm.
        ISBN 0-8050-5174-0
        I. Title.
PS3554.U279W67   1997   97-6884
813'.54—dc21   CIP

Henry Holt books are available for special promotions and
premiums. For details contact: Director, Special Markets.

First published in hardcover in 1997 by
Henry Holt and Company, Inc.

First Owl Books Edition 1998

Designed by Kate Nichols

Printed in the United States of America
All first editions are printed on acid-free paper.∞

1   3   5   7   9   10   8   6   4   2

FOR DOROTHY WALLACE

Each thing is merely the limit of the *flame* to which it owes its existence.

—MAX SCHELER,
Nature et forme de la sympathie

Contents

Acknowledgments

The author wishes to express her thanks to Sandra Dijkstra, Tracy Brown, Greg Robbins, and Catherine Kasper for showing up at *precisely* the right moment.

The Word "Desire"

The Chess Set of Ivory

Chess appealed to my father's delight in quietude, his repressed rage, his trust in institutions, models, and measured behavior. Chess justified what Father liked best: thinking about thinking. He called it: *battling mind*.

Father dwelled in a space of such disembodied quietness his Egyptian students called him His Airship, I believe with affection. Chess allowed Father to make decisions that would in no way influence the greater world—beyond his grasp anyway—and to engage in conflict without doing violence to others or to himself. (Father's fear of thuggery suggested clairvoyance when in a later decade he would find himself undone by a handful of classroom Maoists who called him Gasbag to his face. If clearly they intended to hurt him, they were, admittedly, responding to that disembodied quality of his already evident in Egypt, and his pedantry—a quality rooted in timidity.)

Father was a closet warrior, a mild man and an intellectual, a dreamer of reason in a world he feared was chronically, terminally unreasonable. And he was a parsimonious conversationalist. His favorite quote was from Wittgenstein: "What we cannot speak of we must be silent about." When Father did speak, he spoke so softly that even those who knew him well had to ask him to repeat himself. Once, during his Fulbright year in Egypt, when several of his students had discovered a crate of brass hearing trumpets for sale in the bazaar, they had carried these to class to—at a prearranged signal—lift them simultaneously to their ears. (Yet, in sleep, Father ground his teeth so loudly my mother nightly dreamed of industry: gravel pits, cement factories, brickworks.)

I could add that Father was fastidious, sometimes changing his clothes two or three times a day. He ate little and dressed soberly—if with a specific, outdated flair: on formal occasions he wore a cummerbund. I took after him, played quietly by myself behind closed doors. And if Mother—and she was a big, beautiful Icelander—was a noisemaker, she made her noise out in the world—the Officers Club, for example.

Father once admitted to me that chess saved him from losing his mind—and this was said after he had lost his heart. When he played he became disembodied—a mind on a stalk in a chair, invisible—and if he could keep ahead of his adversary, impalpable, too. In life as in chess, Father did not want to be touched, to be moved, to be seized; he was unwilling to be pinned down or cornered. He jumped from one discourse to another, embracing peculiar and obscure concepts and ideologies about which no one else knew anything; meaningful conversation with him proved an impossibility. In those years chess became the sole vehicle by which he could be reached, or rather, *engaged*—for he could never be reached—the navigable airspace in which he functioned was invariably at the absolute altitude of his choosing. When he embraced the cryptic vocabulary of Coptic gnosticism, he lost his few remaining friends because it was impossible to follow the direction of his thoughts, and that was exactly what he wanted.

In Cairo Father played chess blindfolded and invariably he won. The positions of the pieces on the board were sharper in his mind's eye than the furniture of his own living room (where he was constantly scraping his shins and knocking over chairs).

But I keep digressing. What I wish to write about is a brief period of time in Egypt, one year that seems to stretch to infinity, a year in limbo, a time of disquiet and loneliness. That year was a paradox—both intensely felt and numbing. The world passed before my eyes like an animated stage—distant, colorful, unattainable—and I, in my own little chair, looked on, watchful and amazed, frightened, enchanted, and disembodied, too.

In Egypt, Father had taken to wearing a fez to wander as

unobtrusively as possible. He looked Egyptian—we both did—so that Cairo embraced us unquestioningly, my father's limited but convincing Arabic sufficing during brief encounters with beggars and merchants and dragomen; and he spoke French.

One winter's day on an excursion to the Mouski, we passed the window of an ivory carver's shop, which contained any number of charming miniatures: gazelles, tigers, monkeys, elephants, and the like. As he gazed at the animals—and I supposed that he might elect to buy me one— Father began to cough and hum in a familiar way that meant he was about to make a brilliant move, or was excited by an idea. At that instant a small boy invited us into the shop and offered us two little chairs on which to sit. The carver appeared then, beaming, and sent the boy off to fetch coffee. The tray set before us, the mystery of Father's excitement was revealed: If Father provided the drawings, could the carver make for him a chess set in which the goddesses and gods of the Egyptians and the Romans met face-to-face? Isis and Osiris, Horus and Amon Ra battling Jupiter and Juno and Neptune and Mars? Might sacred bulls confront elephants? He imagined the Egyptian pawns as ibises and the Roman pawns as archers.

This conversation took place in a boil of English, Arabic, and French; already the coffee tray was cluttered with sketches and ivory elephants—examples of sizes and styles. As the ivory carver and my father discussed the set's price and the time necessary for its completion, I sipped sherbet and explored the shadows. I found a stack of tusks as tall as myself and two pails: one contained ivory bracelets soaking to scarlet in henna and the other ivory animals soaking to the color of wild honey in black tea. As I looked the boy came over and with a flat stick stirred the carvings gently, all the while gazing at me with curiosity.

The shop was very old and smelled unlike any place I had ever been; I suppose it was the ivory dust on the air— all that old bone—the henna, the coffee, and the tea. It was a wonderful smell and soothing, so that for several instants I closed my eyes and slept.

When I awoke the boy had vanished, leaving ajar a little door that opened onto the back alley. The alley led to a quarter entirely devoted to leather slippers stained green, and further down an antiques seller's where I had seen a figure of hawk-headed Horus, the god of the rising sun, made of Egyptian paste and the size of a thumb. It had come from a tomb near Luxor.

The little figure had spoken to me with such urgency that, for the first time in my young life, I had dared ask my father that he buy it. He did not take my request seriously. How could a ten-year-old possibly fathom the value of such a thing? Not that it was impossibly expensive—for in those days such pieces were still to be found easily enough on the market. But it was three thousand years old and Father imagined a troubling eccentricity of character: my request seemed excessive. Had I inherited an immodest desire for luxury from my mother, who at that moment was having the hair removed from her armpits with hot caramel? (His own delight in luxury he did not question because compared to hers it was so tame: a collection of chess sets, a few articles of elegant clothing.)

Mother's extravagance and acute blondness were striking anywhere, but above all in Egypt. When in gold lamé she arrived late at a reception at the University Club, a hush descended upon the room. She preferred officers and had befriended a number of the Egyptian brass (including the young Nasser)—handsome men flourishing thick mustaches.

∽

I was learning Arabic. To my delight I discovered if I said *egg'ga* I got an omelette, and *salata,* a salad. Father owned a charming little pocket dictionary with words in French, English, and Arabic, and incongruous illustrations of disparate objects. One page showed a Victorian piano, a British bobby, a sarcophagus, two sorts of cannon, a hula dancer, a radio singer, a caged tiger, a man singing in blackface, an airplane, a hand holding a pen, a pearl necklace, a salted ham, a taxicab, a star, a cobra, and a hat.

Each week my father and I returned to the ivory carver's shop, where the finished pieces accumulated. The Roman castles were Pompeian elephants decked out exactly as in an old print Father had hunted down in the university library; the print was based on a bas-relief uncovered in Pompeii. The little elephants had tusks that ended in spheres the size of small peas. These might be gilded and if they were: should Isis wear a gold necklace and Amon Ra a gold sun? *No.* Father was after simplicity. The Egyptians should be soaked in tea to darken them and this was all.

As he spoke my father fingered an Osiris four inches tall and completed that morning. He had the lithe body of a young, athletic man and the noble head of a falcon. In guise of a crown he wore the solar disc encircled by a serpent, and in his hand he carried the Key of Life. Father said to me: "When Osiris was torn to pieces and his body tossed to the four winds, Isis, his beloved, searched the world until she found every part but the phallus, because it had been swallowed by a fish. She made him another—of precious wood or alabaster, no one knows. Then she laid his broken body on a perfumed bed and embraced him until he was whole again. And here he is!"

Smiling, Father raised the little figure to the sun that in its passage across the sky had suddenly filled the shop with light. Then, under his breath, he said with a bitterness so unique, so unexpected, that I was profoundly startled: *A thing that would not have occurred to your mother.*

Alone on my balcony in the afternoon, I would gaze out over the courtyard below, where Bedouins often camped. I could smell baking bread and hear the children singing. I loved to see the women suckle their little ones, and when the girls danced fearlessly I danced too, for in that quiet air the sound of their flutes and drums readily reached me.

They came because of the public water fountain and an ancient sycamore tree that kept the courtyard shady and cool. At its roots the Bedouins had nested their *goallah* or water pots, and I thought the word wonderful because it contained their word for God. I found a picture of a *goallah* in the *Dracoman,* in a series including the sugarloaf-shaped hat of a dervish and a head of lettuce.

I would also gaze at the beautiful balconies across the courtyard, all pierced with patterns of stars. Sometimes a wood panel slid back and the small face of a child might appear, or that of a woman unveiled, her face impossibly pale, her eyes like the eyes of a caged animal, her throat and wrists circled in silver.

I had left all my toys behind but for a small box of glass and porcelain animals, and a green cloth I pretended was a vast meadow. But I was swiftly outgrowing these things. They paled beside the demands of my own slight body, awakening—I did not know to what, except that when each night I found pleasure beneath my small fingers, pleasure detonating like some sudden star, I imagined a blue man beside me, a blue man with the beautiful face of a bird of prey.

࿊

Today when we arrive to see the finished Osiris, the ivory carver is full of news. Just this morning in Alley of Old

Time, a dervish sliced his belly open and revealed his entrails. A large number of people had gathered beside the carver's shop to throw coins at the dervish's feet and cry: *Allah is great! Praise Allah!* But even more extraordinary, the dervish had spontaneously taken his guts in both his hands and lifted them as though for the carver's inspection, before asking for a needle and thread to sew himself up again. After, he had limped away to die or to recover— "God," the carver says, "alone knows." The blood—and there was very little of it—was not washed away because the spot was considered by some to be holy ground. The ivory carver is eager to show us the blood, but Father at his most imperious says: *"L'extase ne m'interesse point."*

The next hour is characterized by silence, Father examining the new piece with extreme attention, the carver bent over his work—Jupiter—with exemplary intensity. Later on, as we are making our way back to Khan el-Kaleel to hail a cab, we turn off too soon and, wandering in an unfamiliar maze of streets, find ourselves among the butchers' stalls, where Father bumps into a table piled high with several dozen skinned heads of sheep, shining with oil and ready for roasting.

Suddenly I see my father's fez rolling along the street and then Father bent in two and vomiting, spattering the knees of his white linen suit with filth. He vomits violently, in spasms, as little boys looking solemn gather in droves and one stunning man in a white turban offers my father a handkerchief moistened with orange-blossom wa-

ter. Panting, Father grabs this to mop his face and I see a
wild look in his eyes, the look of the woman at the window of stars. Then, somehow, we are in a taxi speeding
home, the generous man whom we will never see again
diminishing like a genie behind us.

Throughout the ride Father's face remains plunged in
the scented handkerchief. When we arrive at our building's
gate, Father raises his eyes and I see that he is still terrified.
He needs help counting change. For a moment he opens
his mouth as if to apologize but says nothing, as though
speaking demands too great an effort. To this day I cannot
smell orange-blossom water without thinking of a cobbled
street, a spoiled fez, my father's stained knees.

Father was ill for two months. A fever pinned him down so
that he could barely move. When he was delirious he raved
that the head of gravity lay upon his heart and that it was
made of oiled lead. He imagined that the Colossi of
Memni had fallen onto his bed and were crushing him,
that his own temple was filling with sand. In the fall we
had seen stray dogs worrying the corpse of a camel. Father
believed he was that camel.

He said he was being pulverized by Time—he spoke as
if Time and Gravity were divine beings who despised him
because he was merely mortal and made of frangible clay;
those were his words: *frangible clay*. Finally—and this happened in May—his fever broke, his mind cleared, his mood

lightened. Father began to mend. Within days we were able to walk to his chamber's balcony, which overlooked the street, to stand together cracking melon seeds between our teeth and tossing sweets to the organ grinder's monkey, who, when the music was over, pulled a tin plate from his pants, and a fork.

The following week Father was back to his desk catching up with his classwork and his correspondence—he was at war with a dozen chess players in other countries. I was "Keeper of the Inkpot." Father teased: Should I spill any, or fail to fill his precious Mont Blanc correctly, I would be shipped off directly to the crocodile-mummy pits of Gebel Aboofayda! (The crocodile-mummy pits were illustrated on page 38 of the *Dracoman,* along with a fountain pen and a straitjacket.)

Now that Father was on his way to total recovery, we returned to Alley of Old Time to collect the completed chess set. It was splendid. Each Roman archer had distinct features, with bow lowered or raised, minute quivers (and these would soon be broken) in place. The stances of the ibises were variable and capricious: One was nesting and another about to take flight. Yet another, poised on one leg, was fishing, and one held a fish in its beak. Isis was very lovely—lovelier than Juno, who had a stern expression and a large hooked nose. Isis had two diminutive breasts; her soft belly was visible beneath the folds of her gown.

After we had admired the set at length and been served

coffee—and I was given a special treat, a square of pink loukoum studded with pistachios and rolled in powdered sugar—the set was placed in its box, wrapped in brown paper, and tied with string. Then, as we departed, the ivory carver displayed a prodigious tenderness for my father by suddenly kissing his sleeve. We stepped out onto the street. It had been freshly watered and beneath the tattered awnings we walked in coolness.

"Before returning home," Father said, "let us pay a visit to the little Horus you once so admired. I imagine it is still vegetating in Hassan Syut's shop." This was such an unexpected delight that for an instant I stopped walking and leaned against my father's side, my arm about his waist.

The Horus was no longer there. It had, in fact, been sold some weeks earlier. However, Hassan Syut had something very unusual to show my father and he went to the back of the shop where he sorted through a multitude of pale green boxes. He returned to the counter with an object wrapped in white linen, and with a flourish revealed a blackened piece of mummy. It was a hand cut off at the wrist, a child's hand carbonized by a three thousand years' soak in aromatic gum. It was a horrible thing, and my father let out a little cry of displeasure, perhaps despair: *Que c'est sale!*

For a reason unfathomable—for still I do not know my father's intimate history—Father was convinced the hand had been offered with malicious intention. "And you still a child," he said. *"Si fragile!"* We were making our way past row after row of green slippers. "Everywhere evil!" I thought I heard him say. *"Partout . . . le mal!"*

His voice was altered; he had begun to bleat as on occasion when he lost patience with my mother, and I, in the still of the night, would hear her return from the mystery that kept her so often away. On such nights it seemed to me that Mother's orbit was like that of a comet. Light years away, when she approached us it was always on a collision course.

Father's words came quickly now; they spilled from his mouth with such urgency I could barely follow: "Evil is a *lack,* you see," I thought I heard him say. "A lack, a void in which darkness rushes in, a void caused by . . . by thoughtlessness, by narcissism, by insatiable desire. Yes, desire breeds disaster. *De toute façon,"* he said now, suddenly embarrassed, "those old bodies should be allowed to rest." I looked into his face. It seemed the hand had designated the darkest recess of his heart and had torn the delicate fabric of his eyes, for his eyes waxed peculiar, distant and opaque: minerals from the moon. I wondered: If a word was enough to create the world, could one artifact from Hell destroy it? The hand, reduced by time to a dangerous, an irresistible density, seemed, in the thinning air, to hover over us.

Father pulled a handkerchief from his vest pocket and pawed at his face. I believe I heard him mutter: "There is no rest." What did he mean? He hailed a cab and I was aware that I dreaded going home.

The cab smelled of urine, and the windows—covered with a film of dust and oil—could not be rolled down, so that we traveled in a species of fog. When we arrived I helped Father from the cab and held the gate open. When was it, I wondered, that he had become an old man?

The elevator was paneled with mirrors and the embrace of infinity vertiginous. I shut my eyes. Stepping into the hall, we heard music, and then, behind the door, Mother's thick voice, her voice of rum and honey, came to us; she was singing: *I made wine . . .*

Father did not ring but instead, holding the ivory chess set against his heart with one arm, fumbled for his keys.

From the lilac tree . . .

He was breathing with difficulty. I feared he was about to die. But the door was open now, and in a room flooded with the full sun of the late afternoon, Mother, her wet hair rolled up in a towel, was dancing, her naked body pressed to the body of a stranger. Seeing us, she held him to her tightly, and, her face against his chest, began to laugh—a terrible laughter that both extinguished the day and annihilated my father and me, severing us from her and from ourselves.

When my father took my hand, the chess set fell to the floor, seemingly in silence so loudly was the blood pounding in my ears. Father held my hand so tightly that it ached, an ache that was the ache of my heart's pain, exactly.

Wormwood

for Steve Moore

Gran'père was dying, and p'tit Pierre stood at the door clutching his cap, clawing at the rim in his terror and excitement. P'tit Pierre was not yet nine and in the light of the lantern his face was very small and white—like a lima bean. M'man ran for her shawl and the two of us set off after p'tit Pierre, who was walking very fast, already a good way ahead. M'man and I were wearing our nightgowns and slippers; we had to walk carefully else stub our toes on the cobbles. M'man called out: *"Allez! Pierre! Pas si vite!"*

It was very dark and foggy. We chased after p'tit Pierre's lantern, which blinked like the Devil in the distance, and once I stumbled. When we reached the gate where Old Owl Head lived in her tiny room above the street, I was frightened and tried to take M'man's hand, but she pulled away. "Slow down!" she yelled at p'tit Pierre again. *"Brigand!"*

Walking as fast as we could, it took us twenty minutes to reach Gran'père's. We could hear his raving even before Margarethe opened the door. I was afraid to go in; the house was transformed by Gran'père's terrible cries. M'man prodded me, her knuckles hard in my back: *"Allez! Allez! Depêche-toi,* Nanu!" We followed Margarethe up the stairs and the closer we got to Gran'père's room, the louder the sound he made. I thought: *What if he's already in Hell?* Pulling back, I collided with M'man. *"Merde!* Nanu!" she cried. *"Je me fâche!"* I hid my face with my hands because I feared she would strike me, but she only pushed me into the room, which was dark except for Gran'père's head lit as if from within by Margarethe's lamp. She set it down on the bedstand beside Gran'père's teeth and offered M'man a chair. Gran'père could have been dead but for all the noise he was making.

"P'pa!" M'man shouted. "P'pa!" Gran'père snorted and smacked his lips. "He's thirsty," M'man decided. Dipping the edge of her shawl into his glass she squeezed some water into his open mouth. "Rah!" he said. *"Oui!"* said M'man. *"C'est moi,* Reine. I'm here beside you: Reine." A strange sound came from Gran'père—like a bullfrog's croaking—so that I laughed out loud. "Nanu!" M'man made a slicing gesture across her neck. This sobered me enough to approach Gran'père. "Gran'père," I said. "It's me, Nanu." Gran'père said, "Nah?" *"Si!"* I said. "Nanu. Your little Nanu." When he did not respond I asked M'man: "Does he know us?" "Shut up!" M'man said. *"Conasse!"* I wanted to cry then so I looked around the room for my own place to sit. I found Gran'père's chair beside the desk where in the old days he went over his accounts. For a time I sat there in the dark, staring at the ugly statuette Gran'père called Wormwood. His nose and tongue and knees horribly protruding, Wormwood was sitting on a stump.

Gran'père was asleep and as he slept he whistled: a sound as monotonous as the wind. Downstairs a clock ticked; I could hear M'man's soft breathing and from time to time I heard her sigh: *"Ah, merde. Merde, merde, merde."* She was almost singing.

On the desk there was a little china vase and because it was too deep to see inside I emptied it into my hand. Some pen nibs tumbled out, two coins, and a key. I slipped the coins in the pocket of my nightgown and examined the key. It was very small and appeared to be made of green brass. I held it in the palm of my hand and, making a fist, squeezed hard. When I opened my hand I could feel the key's impress in my flesh with the tips of my fingers.

Once when I was a tiny child I had asked Gran'père why he kept a thing as ugly as Wormwood around. "If Wormwood were mine," I told him, "I would throw him into the fire." Gran'père said: "Little *idiote!* Wormwood is made of brass and cannot burn. But he has a hot temper: behave yourself, Nanu, or he'll wake up—because yes, even though his eyes are open he is fast asleep. If I decide to wake him, you're finished, Nanu! *Foutue! Foutue!* Fucked, *petite garce. Tu comprends?*"

Remembering this, I bit my lip, but what I really wanted to do was bite Gran'père. I imagined creeping across the room and poking my head under his covers. Before he or M'man would know what was up, I'd have taken a good bite out of Gran'père. And because the room was dark, Gran'père asleep and M'man sleeping too, I stuck out my tongue. I stuck it out so far it touched the bottom of my chin and still I had not stuck it out far enough. Then I saw p'tit Pierre standing inside the door. Made fearless by the dark and the fact that Gran'père was dying, he crept over to me. His mouth hot against my ear, he said, "I saw you! If *le père* Foucart doesn't die I'll tell him! I'll tell him I saw Nanu making faces in the dark. And then I'll watch him give you a good spanking with his shoe."

I said, "I don't give a fuck." P'tit Pierre grinned. He said, "Can I kiss you? You are so pretty, Nanu." I said, "You make me want to shit you are so ugly." P'tit Pierre began to laugh. I could hear him laughing quietly beside me in the dark. Then, crouching down, he waddled like a dwarf around the room, sidling dangerously close to

M'man's chair and Gran'père's bed, looking droll and sinister, too. Once more he was standing beside me. He picked up Wormwood and the china vase, scattering the pen nibs on the table.

"There's a key," he whispered. "Help me find it." I said, "Why? Why should I help you find it? You're nothing but a little thief." I was squeezing the key so tightly my hand was throbbing. "Because," he said, "it's a thing *le père* Foucart showed me." And he imitated Gran'père's voice so well the hair stood up on the back of my neck: "P'tit Pierre! *Viens!* Look at what old Wormwood knows how to do! And better than you, I warrant, little brigand!"

In the dark room, M'man softly snoring and Gran'père whistling like the Devil, I said, "Hush! You sound just like him! I'm afraid! Stop or I'll do it in my pants."

P'tit Pierre fell to his knees and then, his fist in his mouth to keep the laughter deep in his belly, he rolled across the floor. I could hear Margarethe stirring in the house just under us. "Are you going to sleep here?" P'tit Pierre, now at my feet, gazed up at me.

"*Bien sûr!* Idiot! Gran'père is *dying*. I have to stay till he's dead." P'tit Pierre then said very seriously: "Nanu . . . I'll be your husband one day." I said, "*Non!* M'man told me we can't be married because your m'man is a maid who empties Gran'père's bedpan." Hurt to the quick, p'tit Pierre growled: "Your papa has run away! You're no better than a bastard like me." "My papa did *not* run away!" I pinched p'tit Pierre's arm so hard he cried out, waking my m'man. "Hush!" she scolded. "Hush, Nanu. Or I'll burn your tongue in the fire!" But almost as soon as she said this she was asleep.

"My papa is a soldier," I said. "He's fighting the *boche*. When he comes home he's taking me to Holland," I said. It seemed to me p'tit Pierre was crying. "We could elope," I said, "and live deep in the woods on the hill. No one would look for us there. We'll eat berries—"

P'tit Pierre was beaming. "And nuts and wild partridge eggs," he said. "We'll sleep in a big pile of leaves."

"I'll make us a blanket of moss," I said eagerly. "And when we have babies I'll kiss them over and over." As p'tit Pierre looked on I held an imaginary baby in my arms and covered it with kisses. P'tit Pierre bent over me, kissing the air.

"We'll sleep in a bed of roses," he said, recalling a song he had heard in the street. "We'll burn frankincense like they do in church."

"Roses!" I pretended to spit. "Where will you find roses?"

"In Iron Corset's garden," he said gleefully.

"I don't want my m'man's roses," I said, and I pulled his hair.

He said, "I'll make you a bed of fox fur. And when the werewolf comes I'll chop off his head."

"When I am a woman," I said, "I'll run away for sure."

"When I am a man," p'tit Pierre said, "I'll shit without dropping my pants." We both collapsed on the floor, silently laughing. Then for a time we lay together and I could hear p'tit Pierre's heart moving beneath mine.

Because of M'man's violent temper and the injury caused by Papa's departure, to recall the past meant upheaval and isolation. But that night in p'tit Pierre's arms I dared remember an afternoon when Papa and I climbed the hill up to the Bosc du Puy. At the top we rested beneath the ancient trees. We saw a fox pass by, a glassy-eyed rabbit thrown over its back. We saw a snake, green and gold, its eyes gold, moving among the roots and leaves.

Papa was a geologist—he worked for the mines—and that day he told me about the creatures that were buried when the hill was formed. He said we sat at the foot of a tree rooted in a soil black with volcanic ash and the bone dust of woolly rhinos and horses no bigger than cats. He described the water volcanoes of Iceland, the volcanic bombs of Vesuvius, the eruption of Mount Pelée in Martinique caused (or so some said) by an unusual conjunction of the sun and moon. And although it was a story I had heard before, Papa described the whale skull his own father had found digging a wine cellar deep in the yellow clay under rue Dauphine. The famous naturalist Lamanon had rewarded my great-grandfather with a kiss.

"One day I will take you to Holland," Papa had said,

tenderly stroking my hair. "The skull sits alone in a hall of the Teyler Museum." After a moment's reflection he added: "The hall is the size of this wood."

I was roused from this memory, so like a reverie, by Gran'père's snores. They sounded like a knife shaving bone. M'man's snores made the sound of a glue pot simmering. I knew that because once I had helped Papa make glue with the hoof of a horse.

"*Fais-moi peur,* Nanu!" p'tit Pierre whispered in my ear.

"I can't. Not with them so near."

"Yes you can! They are both as good as dead. Start like this: 'The voyage was doomed from the start.'" He nuzzled my neck.

"The voyage was doomed from the start," I began, and p'tit Pierre sighed with pleasure. "A week off the Java coast the ship was swept by plague and all the sailors died."

"The stench was terrible," p'tit Pierre agreed. "All the sailors died but one."

"And this is his story."

"*L'histoire du marin qui se trouvait seul.*"

"All his friends were dead and all his enemies too. And now—"

"Sometimes people die of loneliness, Nanu." Solemnly, p'tit Pierre licked the inside of my elbow.

"Stop that!" I scolded. "You're like a little dog!" He licked me again.

"A lion," he corrected me. "A lion. Lions lick each other. Then what happened?"

"He couldn't manage the ship. The sails were down and he was at the mercy of the tides. There were roaches in the crackers and the water was black."

"He could fish—"

"The fish were all too big to catch. Off Java the fish are as big as elephants."

"He ate shit and he was lonely."

"So lonely one day he shouted into the wind: 'God-damn! I'd take the Devil for a bride!'"

"He shouldn't have said that! Your sailor—*quel con!*"

"He had an inspiration—"

"What's that?"

"He thought: An entire wood was cut down to fill the hold of this ship with sandal, ebony, and cedar. I'll find a nice log and cut off a piece and carve a bride for myself."

"Like Pinocchio! Pinocella! Pinocella!"

"Shut up, idiot. Not like that. You'll see. . . . He took a lantern and made his way down into the hold."

"It was dark and full of rats! God knows what else!"

"Pierre—*tais-toi*. Some logs were loose and rolling. It *was* dangerous down there. But he climbed a pile as high as a hill and looked until he found something he liked. With his ax he hacked away until he had a piece about one meter long. The wood was so hard that each time he struck it he made sparks! And it was as dense as lead. Even his small piece was too heavy to lift. He struggled with it until he lost patience and gave it a kick."

"Saying, 'Goddamn it! Goddamn it! Goddamn it!' "

"The log rolled with the sound of thunder, and when it hit the floor the whole ship shuddered. He scrambled down after it and saw that the log had split wide open. The heart of the wood was green. Green as a corpse."

"I'm *scared,* Nanu. . . ."

"And it smelled queer. But he was a stubborn man. He heaved it up to the deck and began to carve. He made so many sparks he needed no lantern to work by. It took him six days to cut her rough form: her head, her body, her arms—"

"He made her beautiful, Nanu."

"—and it took him seven days to carve her features: her eyes, her lips, her little teeth."

"Thirteen days for bad luck!"

"When he was finished she *was* beautiful. He kept her beside him and at night he held her close."

"He called her Plaisance."

"That's stupid! Plaisance! What are you thinking? No. He called her . . . Amadée."

"Si. C'est mieux."

"Amadée. But, now listen to this, that wood was *strange.* It was the strangest wood in the world. Because even though it had taken him ages to carve her face, hour after hour, her features had a life of their own. Soon his little bride's smile was a sneer. The expression of her eyes changed also. Deep lines appeared—on her forehead and beside her nose and mouth. One morning when he woke up, Amadée was so hideous he threw her away in a corner where the ropes—"

"Coiled like snakes!"

"That night he went to sleep alone."

"Le pauvre, pauvre con!"

"And he had nightmares. In the middle of the night he woke up screaming—"

"A rat! He was bitten by a rat, eh? Nanu?"

"He *thought* it was a rat. Until he lit his lamp and found Amadée back in his bed, scowling like a shark—"

"Green as death!"

"Cold to the touch. Cold—"

"As ice, Nanu!"

"Colder. Cold as *brass*. He picked her up—"

"Although she was so heavy he almost ruptured his kidneys, *le pauvre connard*—"

"—and he threw Amadée into the sea."

"The sea swallowed her up whole! *C'est fini?*"

"*Non.* That night, a strong current pulled the ship back to the Java coast. In the moonlight the sailor saw that the ship was heading toward some immense rocks, so he dropped anchor. But the sea was too deep!"

"*Bottomless!* And Amadée sinking and sinking!"

"Helpless, he watched as the rocks—"

"Shining in the moon, black as Hell . . ."

"—loomed closer. Mountains of black stone."

"There was a sound! Like teeth tearing into the belly of a whale!"

"The ship shuddered and dipped. Water bubbled up everywhere. When the ship rolled over, the logs in the hold broke loose—"

"An entire forest!"

"—shattering the ship."

"Like a matchbox!"

"As the ship sank the sailor was spat into the water. He was crushed against the rocks by the trees that boiled and leapt in the sea. Just before he died he saw Amadée floating past—but fast. Churning the water! Like the Devil speeding back to Hell! But it wasn't Amadée any longer—"

"It wasn't? It wasn't? Who was it?"

"Wormwood."

"Wormwood!" P'tit Pierre took my hand and held it against his heart, which was wildly beating. "*Tu m'as fait grand peur,* Nanu," he said. "I am so afraid!" For a time he was silent, brooding. "Nanu?" he whispered then, his voice tremulous. "He's *here,* in this room with us now!"

"*Je sais.*"

"Nanu?"

"Be quiet now, Pierre."

"How did *le père* Foucart get him?"

"Because he is *evil,*" I whispered.

"Yes, but how did he *get him?*"

"Once a beggar came to the door wanting bread. It was winter and he was near dead with cold and hunger. 'Fuck you!' said Gran'père. 'Why should I give you bread?' The beggar pulled Wormwood out from under his rags. 'I'll give you this for a piece of bread,' he said. 'He's a precious thing . . . very, very old. . . .'"

"And it does a trick! But you know, Nanu . . . *le père* Foucart won Wormwood at the fair in St. Firmat."

The shadows in our corner of the room dispersed for a moment; it was Margarethe, come in with a candle. Looking up I saw her standing over us, her breasts like loaves of good, round country bread.

"P'tit Pierre!" she whispered, bending down and tugging at his sleeve. "Get up and go to sleep! Nanu, you come too. I've made a bed for you in the kitchen." I said, "*Non.* I want to stay here with M'man and Gran'père." "*Bien,*" she said. She took off her shawl and put it across my knees. Then she went to the cupboard and fetched a pillow. When she gave it to me I told her it smelled like sour milk. "Sour milk?" she said. "What will you dream up next? I'm going to sleep for a few hours if I can. *Le père* Foucart has kept me up for two nights in a row. Come and get me, Nanu, when he's near the end."

M'man snorted in her sleep and Margarethe winked. "You'll come for me?" I nodded. My hand ached because I had been squeezing the key. I said, "Margarethe? After he is dead and I am sleeping, will I see his face behind the flames?"

"Only if you are bad, Nanu." She left the room, taking p'tit Pierre by the hand.

For a time I lay there on the floor. Then, because I could not sleep, I went back to the desk and picked up

Wormwood. He was not very large—maybe thirty centimeters tall—but being made of solid brass he was very heavy. It was too dark for me to see where to put the key, so I rubbed Wormwood's base and felt where his toes curled into the bark of the stump; I rubbed Wormwood's skull and ears, and I put my finger into his mouth. At last I found the place—a small hole in Wormwood's back, between his shoulder blades. I slipped in the key and slowly wound Wormwood up. A small sound came from him, a little like the sound a clock makes before it strikes the hour, only far fainter. And then I saw Wormwood's penis—invisible before—rising between his thighs like a great green finger. Slowly, slowly it rose, revealing a majestic set of balls. At that instant Gran'père seemed to crow and M'man, waking, cried out: "What is it?" Springing to her feet, she stood over Gran'père shouting, "What is it? What is it?" I put out my hand to hide Wormwood's penis but there was no need; it had vanished.

Magarethe came running up the stairs and p'tit Pierre too; suddenly there was a commotion in the room as though a flock of birds was feeding there or a flock of sheep on their way to slaughter, bleating. My heart was in my throat and I could think of nothing but winding Wormwood up again. M'man called to me then: "*Vite*," she cried, "*Hurry,* Nanu! Come to your Gran'père's bedside right away, because he is dying. Come here at once, Nanu."

"He's dead," Margarethe said even before I reached

him; and as M'man and I looked on she tied Gran'père's jaw shut with a handkerchief. He looked very odd—as though he'd just had a tooth pulled—and I could tell that p'tit Pierre was thinking the same thing.

Then Margarethe walked to Gran'père's desk. Over-turning the china vase she said: "There were two coins; where are they? Did you take them, Nanu?" M'man shrieked: "Give them back! Otherwise we cannot close his eyes!" and she grabbed me by the arm. Terrified, I pulled the coins from my pocket. When M'man slapped me—and she slapped me hard—the key flew from my hand, flashing once in the lamplight as it fell, flashing once again as it hit the floor.

Roseveine

for Harry Mathews

Our name is Gabriel Temporal-Lux-Blason, son of Hermine Temporal-Lux and Gerard Blason: Phallic Instrument of French Imperialism, for fifty years actively dangerous, gaga for ten and now defunct. As We tackle this memoir, Hermine weeps and Gerard seeps into mud.

Simple names are never good enough and this is why Hermine Temporal-Lux is also called "the Angel of Patience" and Gerard Blason "the Butcher of Madagascar." These designations serve to preface the following: If We are Gabriel Temporal-Lux-Blason, We are also known as "Soft-in-the-Head" (although our head is as hard as yours; We know this having tested it again and again against the Bughouse walls, walls of mortared brick).

We, also known as the "the Lunatic," are the author of unique scholarly works, including "Domesticity as Universal Error," "Cosmic Disorder and the Ordered Domicile," "Delirium as System," "The Inspired Integument," "Birth: A Questionable Event," "The Ideal Uses of the Trochus: An Architectural Manifest," "Reflections on the Fall of Man, the Flood, God's Wrath and an Inventive Solution"; author of an ongoing inquiry into the similarities between the Turritella, the mazurka, the tongue of the anteater, the corkscrew, the soup mill; author of an infinite set of pamphlets, including "Architectural Indications of the Inner Ear," "The Anti-Gravity Domicile," "The Submersible Domicile," "The Quasi-Perpetual Environment," and "An Inquiry into the Structural Limits of Time." (All these fascicles are printed on dove gray Arches and may be had from us for the price of postage.)

∽

If the brain, as We believe, is shaped by thoughts and not the other way around, then our own is composed of one nacreous coil, our thoughts sweeping upward under the influence of a lucent tide, the whole protected by a layering of scales. It is evident that as long as We are living, this supposition cannot be demonstrated. The Memoir, in this instance, must be read as our testament: We wish our skull's contents to be scrutinized by Dr. Aromal with delicacy and exemplary gravity. After, the brain is to be placed in a canopic jar and given to our mother. It is our hope that, should the brain be of ideal conformation, Dr. Aromal will oversee a lithographic series, printed on Arches and prefaced by Aromal's inquiry and our brief paper: "The Brain as the Blueprint of a Transcendent Architecture."

There is no doubt in our mind that it was Père's description of the assassination of the sea tortoise that so addled us initially. The tortoise, its legs caught in a noose, wheels about the boat as gulls circle overhead shrilly piping. When the tortoise is exhausted, a boy (or several, depending on the turtle's size) dives into the water and, seizing it, rolls it into the boat, where it is stunned with a hammer and kept helpless on its back.

Already a fire is smoking up the beach. Hauled to shore, the tortoise is thrust into a pit where, thrashing, he is roasted alive under a heap of burning embers. Père insisted on the quality of the meat—especially the flesh beneath the breastplate. He made this joke: "The tortoise carries his stewpot and coffin on his back. He is called tortoise," Père continued, "because he twists about as he bakes."

We were perhaps five at the time and found the tale odious; that a creature could be cooked alive *in its own shell* seemed especially wicked. We were devastated by the realization that living things were killed to be cooked and eaten, that the ribs of the lamb served as a rack for the meat. "It is the leg bone," Père joked as he carved the Sunday roast, "that gives the dish its shape." Pitiless Père! As he described the turtle feast on the beach, We squirmed

on his lap and looked helplessly on as Death entered the
room and the parlor was metamorphosed into a furnished
tomb. The turtle's anguish, the disgrace of its end, gyred in
our little head. Seeing how frightened We were, how agitated, how pale, Père held us fast and insisted on describing
a market on the Madagascar coast where one may see, set
out on their backs on large tables, living turtles cut from
their shells and lying in pools of blood. This blood is
scooped up by female butchers (also intimately described;
Père had never forgotten the ladies of Madagascar) and sold
to clients who, having brought their own bowls, drink the
fresh blood then and there. Hearing this We began to
squeal but still Père was not done; to tell the truth he had
only just begun. (Where was Mère? In the kitchen over-
seeing the jam-making. This story takes place in berry season.)

Turtle meat is—as you have ascertained—prized in
Madagascar, and now that the turtle is free of its shell and
bellowing, a steak is cut from its breast and then another;
the entrails sliced away, the feet sold next and the liver.
Soon all that remains are its lungs, heart, and head. O
horror! The turtle's eyes are still blinking, its beak opening
and closing. And as if this were not enough to keep a child
from sleeping for the rest of his days, Père now recalled the
head of a decapitated prisoner he had seen when he was
himself a little boy, rolling onto a cobbled courtyard before
being picked up and dropped into a basket. "Its eyes were
open wide," Père said, "and its lips were flecked with

foam. Had it been able to speak, it would have cursed the day of its birth."

Despite his firm grasp, We leapt from Père's knees as though they were red-hot and We hit the ceiling, screaming. This was the first time We blew our stack, and Mère came running with her spoon, her lips sticky with jam. We were on the carpet now, spinning like a top. Père gave us a terrific kick to shut us up and We—reduced to a quivering jelly—were hauled off to our room by Père—thundering like Jehovah, Mère behind weeping, her spoon in the air like a wand, the cook after, and last of all our nurse sniveling into her skirts. As soon as We reached the nursery, We threw ourself under the bed and refused to budge; anyone who attempted to pull us out was bitten. Père insisted We be "let to rot."

It was there, under the bed in the nursery, that little by little We recovered from nervous exhaustion and began to dream of impervious integuments; it was there that our thoughts began to spin like the revolutions of an axle box, preparing the way for our ultimate discovery: the Domicile as Time-Absorbing Cuticle.

Because We proved incapable of formal schooling, We were tutored in the nursery by Monsieur Tardy-Cul, who, whenever We proved testy, warned us that Père had threatened to boil us like a soup bone and who made us wear a heavy wool bonnet with ears even in August, causing our brain to quicken vertiginously and deepening the condition Dr. Aromal diagnosed as *delirious,* brought on by our terror of being devoured by the man the natives of Madagascar called the Meat Grinder. (At this stage, fearing that Père might poison our porridge, We insisted on a food taster, having learned about them in our expurgated *Arabian Nights,* which Tardy-Cul read with an ill-tempered lisp. We also asked for a bodyguard, for We feared if he could not manage to poison us, Père would come upon us as We slept to crush our kidneys with a hammer, or—should he be unable to break the door—send a cobra down the nursery chimney.) We lived in constant fear that at any moment Père would seize us, tear us apart, shove us into his monstrous mouth, grind us to a pulp, swallow us, digest us, and shit us into our very own chamber pot. (We now know that in his accelerating decrepitude Père had forgotten us entirely, consumed by the memories of his exploits in Madagascar: sexual, military, and gastronomic.) The more We were degraded by our tutor and his threats, the greater did Père grow in our mind. Soon there was not an inch in which Père did not crouch fully armed with kitchen knife, cooking pot, and Appetite.

After an epileptic crisis caused by Tardy-Cul's tale of Bruce in Ethiopia who, when looking for the source of the Nile, stood by aghast as sirloins were cut from living cows and eaten raw and fuming, We were rid of Tardy-Cul forever, and all manner of Tardy-Culs thereafter; and, following a minor upset over a governess's tortoiseshell comb, allowed to school ourselves in the tranquil cove of Mère's chamber as she knitted mufflers for the poor and prayed for our health, and where We learned the niceties of class systems, domestic gardens, the names of the colonies, their imports and exports, and, by drawing up lists, to write in a gorgeous hand:

Cochinchine:
The exploitation of forests and mines
The education of silkworms
The fabrication of salt
The exportation of swallows' nests
The importation of opium

One afternoon Mère told us a charming little anecdote that was to be the key to our vision which has ceaselessly inspired us and which prepared us for what was to follow: the visit of Madame Roseveine de la Roulette. Mère told Madame de la Roulette's own story about a hermit crab who, having outgrown his own shell, found an ivory pipe washed to shore and, trying it on for size, took it for domicile. From then on the crab could be seen making its way along the beach, a scrap of seaweed clinging to the stem like a flag. The story made us laugh until We wept; Mère and We made merry deep into the afternoon.

❧

All things of importance have a tendency to inscribe themselves on the sensile pages of our vivid histories. One glorious morning Père was trundled off to Angers to be treated
for phlebitis, colitis, laryngitis, and gouty arthritis. As he
was not expected to return before evening, Madame de la
Roulette was invited for a morning's visit. Because Père
hated her for some reason, We were sworn to silence, de-
lighting in a secret with both Mère and the maid, who was
very gay and winked whenever she caught our eye, quivering with laughter like a greased eel. All this created an
atmosphere of expectation so that the morning of the
Great Adventure, and even before it began, We invented
what We came to call our Dreamful Architecture. With
colored pencils We sketched three worldly domiciles in
which We could imagine dwelling in safety and peace.

That morning We imagined a summer domicile of
sweet grasses, sprinkled with good earth and watered daily.
This domicile is cooled by the natural process of evapora-
tion, a process demonstrated to us by Tardy-Cul and which
until that moment We had deemed of no interest whatsoever. By summer's end this domicile could be harvested. It
came to us to suggest to Heads of State that such dwellings
be manufactured *en masse* for the rustics of tropical climes.

We next imagined a spherical domicile of padded India
rubber so buoyant it could travel the rivers of the world
sans dommage aucune; for example, its front portal snugly

shut, this domicile could navigate waterfalls and rapids without taking in water.

And We invented an airborne domicile with an inflatable roof made of a balloon in the shape of a gently convex mattress that would both keep the domicile pleasantly shaded and protected from the rain, as well as provide nesting places for birds. This domicile looks like a low-flying cloud and its inhabitants dwell far from inquisitous and nefarious eyes. It may be anchored above rain forests and so serve as a platform from which to discover the leafy theater below—animated by birds and butterflies and men: agile tribes who leap from tree to tree with their babes and their pantries strapped to their backs.

At eleven o'clock, Roseveine de la Roulette came to visit, bringing with her a charming collection of shells kept in a large box fitted with drawers. This was carried from her carriage to the summer porch by our man Lagrange. Throughout refreshments We eyed the cabinet with curiosity until, having delicately licked the sugar from her lips, her bodice quivering under the impulse of satisfied *gourmandise,* Roseveine took my hand in hers and led me to the mysterious object of my desire. With soft fingers she pulled the first drawer open and revealed a collection of Turbo shells, "stalwart bodies," said she, "that cannot be torn from the rocks, not even by the strongest hands, nor in the roughest weather." Lifting out a full-bellied, canary yellow specimen, she dropped it in our lap, where it appeared to melt like a knob of butter. She next took up a gold-mouthed Turbo; its interior was the color of egg yolk. That morning We were allowed to hold in both our trembling hands a Turbo marbled green, its nacre shining like the white of a young and healthy eye; a green Imperial parrot Turbo from the China seas; and a violently violet Turbo from New Zealand. Already flushed with excitement, We nearly wept when, the shells returned to their cabinet, Roseveine, her little nails glistening like an intimate nacre, opened a second drawer and initiated us into another world of wonders: spurred Imperators studded with spines, a Delphinula sphaerula as tusked as a tribe of elephants, a tiny trellised sundial from the coastal seas of Tranquebar.

The morning was spelled by Turritella—so like the horns of unicorns—a fantastical harvest of spotted cowries brooding in their cotton wool like the eggs of dragons. The day proved mild, the sun filtered by the lime trees, the air palpable with the sound of bees and Roseveine's silvery laughter. When she was not handing us a shell, she was proffering bonbons in silver paper and although We were but six, we shuddered with rapture, thinking how wonderful it was to share the world with women!

Mère had lunch brought to the porch and because We were so well behaved and Père hours away, his thoughts far from us and ours from him, We were allowed to stay, to continue to hold the shells Roseveine proffered one by one. Enraptured We listened as she, caressing our curls, described the eyes of the cuttlefish "like brown silk shot with threads of gold"; told how she wrote all her correspondence in an ink found in the ink bags of fossil cuttlefish and sent to her from Oxford, England, by a natural historian who wrote books under the pseudonym Aster O'Phyton. This ink needed only to be reduced to a powder and mixed with water to produce a sepia of the best quality. What had precipitated such instantaneous death and fossilization that the ink sacs had not ruptured or rotted? We wished such a calamity upon Père. How We should have loved to see *him* reduced to stone! And when Roseveine described the kraken, its arms the size of mizzenmasts, its suckers the size of pot lids, raking sailors from ships and shell collectors from the coastal rocks, again We imagined Père's instantaneous ruin. However, such revengeful thoughts caused us pain. It was impossible for the Butcher of Madagascar to fall in pieces at our feet: those pieces would reanimate and flourish! Instead of one, a thousand thousand would surge forth and more: a Butcher for each second of the day! For a moment the sky darkened; I heard a beak snapping in the air, a beak studded with an infinite set of teeth. But then Roseveine took up a pearl. It sparkled in her palm like a tiny, pristine world and caused us to smile once again.

Before she left, Roseveine gave us a Voluta imperialis so monumental, so sturdy We declared We should very much like to *live in it*. For at once We intuited: Within such a chamber We might forget that moments are extinguished as they happen, that Time is a famished mouth crushing everything that falls into it (and sooner or later *everything falls into it!*). Already We dreamed of drifting within the smooth coils of a boy-sized shell, of distilling nacre from the blood-soaked air of the paternal Domicile, of living and sleeping in a shallow, navigable room, and of marrying the transmarine Roseveine. We proposed right away and she, bubbly with laughter, drew us to her bosom and kissing our ear murmured: "Sweetheart, I am old enough to be your mother!" (I believe she was but twenty-five at the time.) Her smell of ambergris was new to me and our infant birdling rose for one thrilling instant and briefly piped—for what exactly? We could not have told you.

That night, and once We were adrift in our little bed, a bed in the shape of a scallop, and, thanks to a tantrum, suspended from the ceiling so that it could be reached only by a rope ladder, Roseveine's green turban, her horned Murex and shimmering Tritons, her true labyrinths and false cornucopias, swiftly, silently orbiting in our mind's eye, We began to dream our Dreamful Architecture of Unfulfilled Desire, which, in time, evolved into the Ideal Architecture of Fulfilled Desire: the prodigious marriage of aesthetics, chemistry, and psychiatry. As snug as a cephalopod in its retreat, our ladder coiled at our feet, We began to seriously investigate the Domicile as a Sanctuary in which to float far from the blustering winds of patriarchy, the sounds of bells, of kitchen chatter, the horrible ring of the telephone recently installed.

The Voluta pressed to our lips, the words We had heard for the first time tumbled about in our brain like bits of green glass at the bottom of the sea: *coral zone, coralline, littoral; annelids, ammonites, and zoophytes* . . . Yes, these lovely words and also certain phrases she had whispered into our eager ear such as *obscure crevices* and *lonely places; deep waters, the sand under stones; muddy bottoms, the Sea of Aral, stalk-eyed crustacea, gardens in penumbra, rafts of tropical debris; the herring fleet at Wick Bay, tiger cowrie* . . .

We were roused in the middle of the night by Père who in his pain and fever imagined himself in the thick of the wars in which he was such a devastating player; the years in Madagascar when from Majunga to Tananarive, the roots of trees were gorged with blood and all the earth blackened by the dead. His pain was great; he could not move his bloated legs but only thrash his arms and hack at the air with his sword and shout: "I am the Kingdom and the Glory!" We could not help but hear him and, plunging beneath the covers, weep. It came to us that the world is far too corrupt to have given occasion to the gentle mollusk, and imagined it an asteroid fallen from some other universe.

༄

Because of Père's incapacity—he kept to his bed as though fixed there with glue—Mère invited Roseveine to luncheon the following week. Père, propped up with pillows, was polishing the pistols that had served him in the wars, all the while shouting at phantom whores and soldiers. From time to time his voice floated out to the porch where We sat in the shade of the lindens served by the maid nearly doubled over with suppressed laughter. Indeed it seemed a daring thing to be making merry on the porch with a woman whose company Père had forbidden, whilst Père, confined to his chamber, engaged in phantasmagorical fornication and war.

We were served an ethereal lunch: a salad of nasturtiums, squash blossoms made into beignets, an orange-flavored flan—the whole washed down with rare Chinese tea. Whenever Père's ranting would reach us, Roseveine bubbled over with laughter. On one of these occasions We took the liberty to slip from our chair and, concealed by the tablecloth, to take one of Roseveine's slippered feet in our hands.

"And what are you up to, little husband?" said she, gently teasing. "Playing at cobbler?"

"Yes!" We replied, although it was a lie. "That is what We are doing. We are playing at cobbler!"

"A *royal* cobbler, apparently," she said laughing to our mother, "who refers to himself with a royal We! But I would have it no other way," said she. "In other words, if I am to be cobbled, well then: cobble me royally!"

Reassured by this, We unlaced the slipper to find a little stockinged foot, deliciously damp, smelling of live oysters and raw silk. With trembling lips We caressed her toes. We heard Roseveine sigh. With a tinkle her custard spoon fell to its dish.

"The flan is delicious," Roseveine said to our mother, "and so is your little son." Bending over and peering down under the table she smiled at me meltingly and with her hand caressed my cheek. For one dizzying instant she probed my ear with her little finger. "Your ear is exactly like a Bulla ampulla," said she.

So touched were We our eyes welled with tears. "Little husband!" cried Roseveine as We nibbled her instep, "I have fallen in love and decided to divorce Monsieur de la Roulette and—with your mother's permission—marry you!"

We grabbed her calves, and our face pressed to her knees, clung there like a modest echinoderm *sans* the instinct to travel. For a long moment We stayed there, our thumbs pressed to the rotator bones of her ankles.

But this charmed moment was interrupted by a roar from Père, the shrill voice of Père's nurse, a seismic thudding that seemed endless and held us frozen in terror and surprise, and then the sudden appearance of Père himself seething with rage and nearly busting from his bathrobe and Moroccan slippers. Anchored to the doorframe and with all the strength he could muster, Père, visibly approaching exhaustion, bellowed:

"What is that Jewess doing here?"

Again Roseveine's laughter percolated through the air.

Standing to face him, she gathered her skirts to her bosom and spreading her legs pissed profusely, her amber water a stunning spectacle recalling the engravings We had seen of the Victoria Falls on the Zambezi and Tisisat on the Blue Nile. Not surprisingly, her piss had the smoky fragrance of Lapsang souchong. This sublimely anarchic act hurtled Père into the vortex of apoplexy; he did not survive the afternoon.

But this she could not know. For as Père, brittle as mummy, crumbled to his knees, his hands splashing in the steaming puddle she had made, Roseveine sailed off and away, down the balcony steps, into the garden, past the stone fountain, the banks of trees, into the pergola and out the garden gate. She created a void that has never been filled, not even by the persistent memory of her laughter.

Several months after Père's demise, Roseveine came to visit one last time. She and her husband were about to leave France for French Canada, where they intended to form a publishing company devoted to the Natural Sciences. Their first publication would be Aster O'Phyton's *Ocean* illustrated with lithographs, some of which she had brought along to show me: *A Fleet of Medusae, Tubipora Musica,* and one which caused us to cry out in terror but also in secret delight: *A French Officer Seized by a Gigantic Cuttlefish.*

It was early fall and warm enough to take tea outside. Seeing our profound distress, Roseveine took us into her arms and whispered: "Little husband! You must know my heart is like a living shell, a domicile in which you shall be kept, always." She told us to put our ear to her heart. "Listen!" said she. "Do you not hear the sound of the ocean?"

∽

The Ideal Domicile affords its occupant an exquisite state of submerged quietude and more: inside and out it reveals a known pattern which—because of the dramatic change in scale—is simultaneously reassuring *and exciting!* As in nature, each Domicile contains a secret and subtle variation known only to the inhabitant and dependent upon his own corporeal dimensions and aesthetic or spiritual sensitivities. Like a sacred text that has been copied out again and again by a fallible scribe, each domicile is subtly idiosyncratic.

After years of intensive reflection, one decided upon the Trochus: it is ubiquitous and extremely pleasing to the eye—bringing nothing so much to mind as the Babel towers of Ur. Its principal spine is often edged with a handsome series of protective spines, its walls so thick as to be nearly impenetrable, its inside sumptuously nacreous.

Within the confines of the Ideal Domicile, one may contemplate—*with growing disinterest*—the cyclical seasons of human emotion. One's thoughts circle with minor variations and, as reverie is reduced to a cumulative mirroring of spiraling space, worldly velocities still to a snail's pace. The universe, silenced, diminishes progressively until it vanishes altogether. The occupant is reduced to an embryo, a mollusk: *to reverie itself.* A confusion slowly sets in between inner and outer environments, and, one glorious morning, one awakens spiritually fused to the shell. The shell, no longer exterior to the self, *becomes the self.* One's identification with the integument is complete. The spiral spells the soul's intimate architecture; time and space— those most cumbersome of cuticles—cease to impinge upon the dreamer.

Had one not learned of Her return, surely one would still be blissfully suspended in that state of disembodied delight. But Mère's message, knuckled in Morse code upon the hull, roused us from our reverie. One was eighteen and had never known love, only the memory of love. Slowly one unwound one's blood, painfully stirring after many sluggish months, and it came to one at once, without any deliberation, that one must create a bower in order to coax the beloved into the Domicile. Just as the bower bird of Madagascar sets out shells, and seeds and flowers, to entice his mate into the nest, so would one construct an irresistible portal leading into the Domicile. (Indeed, as if this had always been kept at the back of one's mind, the Chamber was big enough for two.)

The fact is that the knowledge of Roseveine's return produced an upheaval in one's brain of stellar velocity. Yes, one admits to the obsessive indulgence of an impossible plan that in a trice had one's brain wound so tightly its unwinding was inevitable. Armed with the largest wheelbarrow one could find, one scoured the countryside for beautiful things with which to construct the Bower, the Bower to coax the Beloved into the Domicile, transformed to Bridal Chamber.

The Bower took the form of a sea grotto; one used pink mortar to arrange the baptismal fonts and basins. These things are all in the form of scallop shells and carved of Italian marble: pink, red, green, and blue. We also uncovered an altar in a small church near Angers decorated with helixes and pectens, and even a chalice formed of a nautilus shell. Pearl buttons abounded in the closets and dressers of my nearest neighbors—as did pearl brooches and rings. It never occurred to one that these borrowings in the name of longing were, in fact, Thievery! One thought only of the bride, you see, and one's wish to stun her.

Before one's work was completed, one was seized, dunked into a *camisole de force,* and brought to the Buggery, where one must navigate edges, eat slop, and listen to the rantings of one who believes he is Bonaparte and the other Sheikh Ibrahim Ibn Abdullah. For three months now they have been fighting for Egypt. The room one shares is a perfect square, one's pallet rectangular. Each man keeps to a corner; the fourth corner belongs to the spider. She affords one's only silent entertainment. Her Domicile is a place of untold thuggery.

Das Wunderbuch

. . . A nd there is that other thing, perhaps of no importance in terms of Annie's suicide, and yet I cannot help but think of it because of its place in the family history. I am speaking of the martyrdom of my father's brother, Maximin Blanchetière, killed in his own orchard by the Lecoy brothers.

In 1888, Maximin wrote a letter to the local paper denouncing the use of chemical pesticides and mocking the archaic systems still popular in our countryside such as paying the vicar to excommunicate caterpillars—a thing the Lecoys had done. At the trial the Lecoys blamed Maximin for the ruination of their gooseberry bushes by a midsummer invasion of Abraxas grossulariata. They testified that

Maximin was a Satanist who raised caterpillars and locusts by magical means. The truth is that Maximin raised swallowtail butterflies. The Lecoys reasoned: *If june bugs, moles, and crows are all beasts of Satan, and Maximin Blanchetière protects them, then Satan is Maximin Blanchetière.* A witness at the trial, Eustache Pot, told how once when his bakery was plagued by cockroaches, Maximin had brought him a large hedgehog. Madame Pot threatened to leave her husband if he didn't give the hedgehog back at once. In the scramble the hedgehog bit Madame Pot on the chin.

This is how the murder took place: Gaston and Gontran Lecoy ambushed my uncle in his orchard the evening of July 3, 1889. Although Maximin was as strong as two bulls, they wrestled him to the ground. Then Gaston Lecoy broke Maximin's head with a hammer. They left him lying there but after several hours returned. When they saw that Maximin was still breathing, Gontran kicked him several times in the head. One of my uncle's eyes flew out of its socket and it is said that this drove Gontran mad. He was always something of an idiot, but the sight of Maximin's eye staring at him from the grass robbed him of human language. At the trial Gontran could only bray and nod his head. Gaston did all the talking.

The night of the murder, Maximin's body was brought into the house, washed, and laid out on clean linens in his very own bed. Maximin's face was hidden, incongruously, beneath his Sunday hat, and his head was concealed by bandages.

Retelling this story eighty years later brings two things to mind. The first is that there is a stained-glass window in the village chapel depicting Saint Radegund crushing bugs beneath her feet. The second is that as children we believed for every lizard we killed we'd spend one hundred years less in Purgatory. When I was a girl I was terrified of eternal damnation, so terrified that when I became a woman I could never be alone with a man. That's why I never married, even though I fell in love. His name was Roger Poulet. He finally gave up on me and went to fight the German swine. They say he died just like a bug, his legs torn from his body.

There was a song we children used to sing:

> *Bad mole, ugly mole*
> *Leave p'pa's garden alone*
> *or p'pa will burn you, beard and bone.*

In the old days we did *coulinage*. We'd do this in February: go into the orchards with torches on a night of full moon and singe the bark of all the trees to burn away the little eggs and the lichen. After the *coulinage* the entire village would go to Vieux Noë's house for pancakes and hot cider. Despite the cold we'd eat outside with the full moon and the torches lighting up our plates and faces. And we'd dance! Even the children would dance. I loved it when Maximin held me high off the ground and pressed me to his chest—I was only six when they broke his head open, you see. We could turn around and around and the moon and the torches would make a ring of fire—that is how it seemed: a ring of fire.

After Monsieur Teste came to town with his free pamphlets, his bottles, and his portable music machine, Maximin was the only one to hold to the old ways. He'd torch his field, light bonfires to attract the moths and kill them, and he'd burn sulfur, too. Surely the smell of sulfur had something to do with the Lecoys' conviction that my uncle was the Devil.

Imagine with me for a moment, if you will, a stone house, ancient and low, with a root cellar and a cobbled courtyard. A poor, simple farmer's cottage of four rooms only; a house with walls green with moss there where the stones are not green with ivy; a house with a hook over the door for pulling bundles of lime tree leaves up into the attic for drying. There are chinks in the stones where grass grows, and here and there a stalk of ripening wheat or a scarlet poppy. Imagine a house heated by one wood-burning stove, a house that smells of saltpeter and pot-au-feu; imagine a kitchen strung with queerly shaped cooking pots from another time, a bookshelf that bends beneath the weight of a few old, very old books—the library of three generations. Once Maximin Blanchetière's house, it now belongs to my brother, Henri: it is the house where Annie was born, and where she lived until her marriage to Charles Bouchot.

Annie's favorite book was one she could not read because it was written in German. It is a book Roger Poulet acquired during World War I—I do not know how—and sent to me. It is called *Das Wunderbuch* and if you open it— as I am doing now—you may see, as clearly as if they were laid out on the table before you: the bones of the hand, the vocal chords of a bullfrog, the musculature of the cobra's head in erection, the embryo of a crocodile sleeping in its egg. And you may see other marvels of nature such as the geysers at Yellowstone Park in America, an African baobab shading a tribe of elephants; and you may see the pyramids of Egypt and the Tower of Babel.

The frontispiece of *Das Wunderbuch* is a pen-and-ink drawing of an alabaster bas-relief of King Ashurnasirpal worshiping the sacred tree of the Assyrians. A winged god hovers over the tree as if to bless it. Not too long ago, when Annie was thirteen and we were in the kitchen together peeling apples, she put down her knife and sighed. I asked her if she was in love. She said, "Yes! I am in love with King Ashurnasirpal!" And she laughed her wonderful laugh as clear as water. Looking at his image now I must agree: he is the most beautiful man I have ever seen or ever will see. "This book was given me by the one man who loved me and the one man I ever loved," I told Annie. "It is the one gift he gave me and then he died, torn apart like a bug. If I had married him he would be alive and I would not be living in my brother's house, but in a snug little house of my own, my garden full of roses." She said then: "But don't you love Papa's house? Don't you love Papa's fruit trees and your room, so sunny throughout the day? Don't you love us?" she pleaded with me then. And, of course, I did. I loved them all and still love them even though Annie is dead and buried these twelve months and Henri and Simone are only ghosts of their former selves.

Dear Annie. Such a fortunate child, coming late in a marriage of love, and having been brought up in luxury— not riches, mind you, but the luxury of tenderness, of simplicity: clothes carefully mended over and over again, meals prepared from garden vegetables, fruits from her father's orchard, and eggs gathered from nests made by the hens she had named: La Rousse, Rosette, Toujours Caca, Lili. The white goat, Docile, still gives a rich, sweet milk from which Simone once made a prodigious cheese. And Henri's kitchen garden filled the house with the smell of rosemary and thyme throughout the entire summer.

When things have vanished, or have been irretrievably altered, and one is far from happy times, far from the people and places that mattered, it is surprising what remains in the mind—sometimes the oddest things. Annie running in with Lili's first egg. Henri fixing Maximin's chair. Simone wiping her hands on her apron and saying: "I wish to Hell everybody'd just sit down!" It is the simplest people, I mean the ones who are not complicated, whose minds are not occupied elsewhere, who matter. I think I am fortunate because the people who mattered (and matter still) are the members of my own family. That is not always the case. For example, Simone always made me feel at home even though at times I exasperated her. Then again, like mothers-in-law, sisters-in-law exasperate no matter how hard they try not to. Mostly, though, Simone and I were at peace, at least we were never at war, and better still, we were often friends. I would share the chores, cook the things she did not know how to make—the dishes Mémé Normandy had taught me. Or we would have egg contests. One week we cooked *œufs à la Beaumont* with artichokes and asparagus, *œufs Bercy* with sausage, Polignac eggs, and Simone's own *à ma façon*. I thought Simone and I should put our wits together and write a cookbook, call it *The Norman Val de Loire* and include Loire River pike poached in cider, Norman duck roasted with Anjou pears. As you can see, it is not only people I love but the food we shared. Here in Milly I get pap: milk soup and eggs scrambled to inconsistency—although my teeth are as strong as ever. I can't hear much, I strain to see, but I can bite and chew with the best of them. "Give me a chicken wing!" I tell them. But no—they fear I'm so gaga I'll choke. If you *cared* for us old folks, I say, you would cook Annette potatoes for us and grilled chicken *à la diable*. You should be thinking of God, is what they tell me, not chicken *à la diable.* But for the old, eating well is our one, our only pleasure. That and remembering those we continue to love.

Writing all this down in a little room that always smells like sour milk, my possessions reduced to the little I could pack into a suitcase and carry, I recall the child Annie, *ma mie,* as though she were here beside me; recall her gentle ways—for she was the light of our lives and when that light went out the world grew dark. Forgive me. How can I help but to weep a little?

Annie always had a green thumb. A tiny child, she planted sunflowers in little plots surrounded by pailfuls of white river stones. She was three or four. Later she would become famous for her radishes. Simone taught her how to make cheese, her fresh *crémet.* Annie rolled hers in flakes of pepper: black and red.

Her father taught her how to prune trees, to degerm potatoes for the winter; how to save carrots in sand. They picked the apples and pears together, packed the truck for market. She spent her summers in the orchard beside him, or in the gardens on her knees; autumn evenings we all sat together weaving garlic, onions, and scallions into garlands, selecting the fattest seeds for the spring planting, scouring the copper pans with sorrel leaves and salt. I recall Annie's solicitous concern for stray cats, scarabs, and lizards. The bowls of milk she put out for the hedgehog. Her collection of owl casts. The first time she put on lipstick. The first time Charles came by.

Annie was not more than a child when the courtship began—and this may explain in part, surely not entirely, what happened, or rather why certain things, irremediable things, happened. Something in her broken and in him, broken—although many say he was already broken, *fêlé,* in other words: cracked. She was sixteen—all elbows, knees, and wrists, the tallest girl anyone had ever seen.

Early in the courtship Charles took Annie to the gardens near Milly. The valley had been suffering drought for five years and many of the larger trees, planted in the middle of the nineteenth century, were dying. The ivy that bordered the paths was spare and the lake at the garden's center only half its usual size. These things distressed her. When living things suffered she had a way of shrinking a little and Annie moped along the paths until the sight of a fat toad caused her to call out with joy—a cry Charles misunderstood. As it lumbered toward them, blinking in the sun, Charles crushed it with the heel of his shoe.

Annie ran from him then and, because she hated Charles now, knowing hatred for the first time—of this I am certain—she left the path to hide from him; stealing up a little hill clustered with camellias, she crouched down and vanished. The ground was dry, covered with sand— how ordered the garden was! And so she settled down among the leaves prepared to spend the afternoon. She knew that once her father had heard what Charles had done he would scold him.

Charles searched for Annie all over the park. He thought her behavior was unreasonable, maddening, childish, and also somehow charming. The incident amused him almost as much as it angered him. That he had hurt her for the first time exhilarated him, and once when he called her name he laughed out loud. But when he had explored all the paths and still did not find her, he became enraged with what he would call thereafter her muleheadedness. He tore a branch from a lilac tree and impatiently thrashed the trees and shrubbery and the gravel path. On the drive to her father's house Charles imagined giving Annie a slap and then a kiss. He imagined penetrating Annie for the first time.

Although Henri's house was charming, Charles saw only that it was poor. He despised the old table covered with an oilcloth and displaying the cut-glass vase Henri had won for Simone at a fair. The room was always filled with potted geraniums—a scent Charles loathed—and it smelled a little of Henri's compost heap, too.

Henri was not at home, but Simone was. Charles found her outside feeding the hens. When Simone saw Charles she blushed; her apron was dirty and her hair tied back with a rag. Simone liked Charles and was flattered by the attention he paid her daughter. Charles had inherited thirty thousand trees and that made him a very rich man.

Before her marriage to my brother—and it was a marriage of passion—Simone had been the wife of a pharmacist and so knew herself to be far better than a gardener's wife. If Henri was still handsome and virile at sixty and—if unschooled—tremendously smart, he was, after all, little more than a peasant. When she had been the wife of a pharmacist, Simone's table was covered with linen. At the center stood a fine copy of an old Chinese bowl. Not a piece of bric-a-brac won at a fair!

Simone wished Charles had not seen her feeding maggots to hens. She wanted to tell her daughter's suitor about the things she had left behind for love, the gold-rimmed fruit dishes, the feather-trimmed slippers she'd tossed at the pharmacist's head the morning she'd moved out without a pot of cold cream to her name.

Simone was enraged with Annie. "For God's sake!" she cried, pulling the rag from her head and smoothing her hair. "The child eats frogs' legs! Why the tantrum over one dead toad?" She told Charles to take a chair at the round table—they had no other place to sit—and to wait for her while she pulled a comb through her hair and slipped on her shoes. "What a baby she is," Simone said of her daughter, and when she returned she poured us all a glass of lemonade. "But you mustn't take her little *crises* seriously." As Charles drank, Simone watched his throat. She thought him perfect—although he was not—and imagined Annie serving pie to doctors' wives on *Moustiers*.

When Henri returned, he and Simone went off together to search for their daughter. Charles insisted on staying behind; he was at a loss and unsure now if, in fact, he wanted to court such an impossible creature. Henri had explained to him that as a little girl Annie could recognize all the toads in the garden and had given them names. "Richelieu is sitting under the pump right now," Henri said. "Shall I introduce you?" Simone gave Henri a look. "She calls them her *drôles*," said Henri.

Charles watched Henri and Simone climb into the truck. He sipped his lemonade and thought about what he should do. While I fed the hens, Charles examined the family pictures in their cheap frames and then began to explore the house. With growing excitement he entered Annie's room. It was just off the kitchen, with a view of the kitchen garden and, beyond, the orchard. Annie had grown up with that view of trees—apple, plum, and pear—and the one thing she had liked about Charles—and this before she met him—was his father's trees. They could be seen from the road rising up the hillsides in perfect rows. In spring those hills in flower looked like paradise. When Charles first introduced himself at a dance and told Annie that he owned those trees, she—who had that day seen them in the spring light blooming like a sea of foam— looked at him with interest. "You could raise bees!" she told him. "All that nectar! All that pollen!"

Now Charles looked out on Henri's trees. Each one was admirably pruned—Henri was something of a genius with trees—and these were the most graceful Charles had ever seen. And they were laden with fruit.

Annie's little bed was covered with a starched chenille spread, so worn as to be almost transparent. Her dresser top displayed the usual clutter: a musical jewelry box containing communion memorabilia and a few Roman coins she had found while working in the gardens. The room had no closet but instead a small armoire and when he opened the door Annie's cotton nightgown brushed against his face. I imagine that the sweet smell of her body, both green and ripe—something like honey, something like vinegar— caused him to groan, to take the cloth in his fists and bury his face. This is how Annie found him.

She had hitched a ride with one of the locals and because Charles's car was parked in front, she had taken off her shoes and stolen into her room from the kitchen. Amazed, Annie stood on her room's threshold and saw Charles standing with her nightgown crushed to his face. He appeared to be sobbing. And then he turned, and seeing her fell to his knees in confusion—a gesture he had once seen in a movie. She had shamed him; he felt like a child caught stealing. He was a little child on his knees fearing his father's wrath and he said to her, as though he was a little boy about to be whipped, "Forgive me." And because she stood over him—lovely, damp in the heat of the day, lips parted in amazement—Charles reached up and kissed her, his confusion masked by his need for forgiveness, his senses assaulted by the earthy smell of her hair and her skin. Her tongue tasted like peaches. The kiss took Annie by surprise—she had never before been kissed—and there in her little room where she had so often dreamed of love, my niece melted. The kiss convinced her that she was in love, or at least that she was supposed to be in love. This is how I imagine it. Then it was Charles's turn to flee.

How bare her cupboard had been! Work pants, the man's shirt she wore to market hanging from a hook, the few skirts and blouses she had worn to school, and her one party dress—something of Simone's. Let out at the hem it looked frumpy and dated. Inspired for the first time in his life, Charles drove to Milly and bought Annie a dress— something for the late summer, flowery, made of crêpe de chine. Even on sale it was fantastically expensive.

Before any of us knew what was happening, Annie was wearing that dress and Charles had come for dinner. And as Annie cleared the table and Simone sliced the cobbler into five equal slices, Charles and Henri talked about trees, the many varieties Charles's father had planted before he died. Would Henri come and look the plantation over and give Charles the advice he so desperately needed?

Annie was thinking: *If I marry Charles it will be like this, with the five of us together speaking of trees and gardens.* Later, when she brought the coffee in on Simone's wicker tray— a thing so old and ugly I could weep just thinking about it—Annie caressed Charles's neck shyly with her hand.

When he responded by playfully slapping her rump I thought, *Ah! Merde. J'aime pas ce con!*

Now I wonder: Had Annie not been with her father that summer but instead active with others her age, someone might have said: You're going out with Charles Bouchot? *Ce con?* And it would have been enough to save her. *Ce con?* The bubble would have burst and Annie would have seen, thanks to that simple phrase, just where she was headed: sharing the fleeting years of her life with a boor.

I recall how Annie, briefly, dreamed of more, of continuing her studies so that she could master the new techniques she read about during her one brief year at agricultural college. Once, she'd startled us all by raising her fist to the sky and shouting: "Imagine a radish this big!" She dreamed up purple asparagus too, and pink eggplant. "They have blue corn in America," she told us, impressing us with her new knowledge. Blue corn! Was Henri proud or worried when he said, "Already she knows more than I!" "Stay with me next year," Henri said also. "Help me for one more year. Then take up your studies again if you still want to." Thinking of this I find I am angry with my brother.

Simone once said something touching and unexpected. She said her life with Henri was like Penelope's weaving: she was always in the process of unweaving and reweaving. She said: "Even now I tear out the old patterns. But it gets easier. Things are simpler, now." And she said: "Henri has made me a happy woman. He takes my body with both his hands—the same way he raises a piece of fruit to his lips. Like a hungry child! With both his hands!"

At that instant I loved Simone as I had never loved her. I dared speak my mind: "Simone! What if Charles needs to be torn out, too. Let's take our scissors to Charles!" You would have thought I had uttered a blasphemy.

I was right, of course, and Simone should have listened. If she had, Annie would still be with us. And because Simone knows this, she never comes to see me. If she did I would be grateful, because I want to talk about Annie. I want to reminisce. And talk would be good for my brother, Henri: it would do us all good to remember.

There is one last thing that comes to mind and I don't know how it fits. But something terrible happened to Annie when she was fourteen and although she was not at fault, she was crushed by remorse for a very long time. It was something she couldn't forget and I think it made her vulnerable, somehow.

This is what happened: It was summer. Annie took her bicycle and went to the river to a place she especially loved because it was here that she and Henri had spent many quiet afternoons fishing for crayfish and freshwater eel. That day Annie was joined by her best friend, Isabelle

Tricot. They were a frisky pair, full of fun and aware—if only recently—of just how pretty they were.

The river Loire is only about one quarter of a mile across at that point and when the girls saw a group of boys walking along the far bank they stood to get a better look. And because the girls felt safe—protected by all the swift water—they responded when the boys called out to them. It was childish banter. "What are your names?" The girls gave false names. "Where do you live?" They made up a place: "Le Bout du Monde!" they cried. The End of the World! "How old are you?" "Old enough to know!" the girls answered. "What do you know?" The boys' excitement was irresistible. "How to talk to boys!" Isabelle and Annie were laughing wildly. This was their first flirtation, and from where they stood the boys looked tall and dark and limber. The novelty delighted them all.

But then one of the boys dove into the river and started across. Isabelle and Annie were astonished and they were impressed—the Loire is treacherous, thick with undercurrents and shifting banks of sand. The boy was foolhardy—of that I have no doubt—and he should never have attempted it.

Isabelle and Annie found themselves caring deeply about the heroic, foolish, wonderful boy, and they stood by the water transfixed as he swam toward them, gathering speed. They were excited and frightened, too, and holding on to one another they cried out, "Oh! What will we do?

Oh God! Oh God! What will we *do?*" It was then that
they saw his body roll to the right before sinking; the boy
had vanished and his friends were shouting his name:
"Didier! Didier!" One of the others entered the water, but
gingerly—he did not dare swim too far out. He, too, was
calling: "Didier! Didier!" For an instant Didier's head was
visible downriver. No bigger than a berry, it appeared only
to vanish again near the old mill, there where the river
makes a sharp turn. They were all running now, the girls
on one bank, the boys on the other, hoping to catch sight
of Didier. But he was lost now, never to be seen alive
again. His body, bloated and swarming with beetles, was
found weeks later among the tall yellow irises that grew
around the mill's foundations.

Annie and Isabelle mourned the dead boy, but it was
Annie who dreamed of him. Sometimes in her dreams his
face would surface from a black water, a face so beautiful it
would cause her to wake up gasping for air, submerged
with longing. (And Didier was beautiful. His photograph,
put to porcelain, is visible on the grave.) Sometimes she
dreamed it was she who found the body rotting among the
yellow irises, his body black and green, swarming with
butterflies. Once, horribly, she dreamed that when his face
rose from the black water he opened his mouth to speak,
and an eel spilled out and fell across her knees.

Annie went to Didier's funeral. When she approached
his mother, the woman turned away and spat. Two years
later, when Charles began to court her, Annie dreamed

that Charles had swum from across the river, and that he dragged the Tree of Life behind him. Annie believed Charles was offering her his life, that somehow he was himself the gift of life. But I believe that Annie was already dying and that the dream was a warning. I believe that the tree was Annie, and that Charles had torn her up by the roots, you see. He was dragging her behind him, God knows where.

Lovemaking with Charles had left her confused and wakeful. It was as if her own desire frightened him. Yes, that is what I imagine: Annie's desire frightened him. Lying in a new bed in a room that smelled of a store, Annie longed for her father's house, to be the child she was but a month before—listening to the rafters creak in the wind of a summer storm in a room that smelled of the passing seasons and of her own old garden clothes.

Annie died in this way: She walked into Charles's forest until she was somewhere near the center, until nothing was visible but the sky and branches reaching out in all directions. This was early autumn and the air was rich with the scent of fruit. Annie chose a place. Then she took a pruning knife from her basket and cut both her wrists so deeply it is hard to imagine how she did it except that she may have held the knife between her knees. Then she lay back, her head in leaves and earth, and she died looking up at the sky. Charles found her late in the day because of the crows.

Here in Milly, they've asked me to stop talking about it because it was depressing everyone. But I can't stop thinking about it. And I can't help but think this: If I could understand, if I could see how we were all at fault—and this despite our love for her (because it is true that she was the apple of our eyes)—then Henri would rise from Maximin's chair and go into the garden and begin pulling weeds, and Simone would drop by here to see me—if only for a moment—and I would be able to sleep and to dream again.

In *Das Wunderbuch* there is a picture of the camphor gatherers of Sumatra. The camphor tree is sacred because it is the earthly mirror of the Tree of Fate. Deep in the woods it hides, and in dreams reveals itself to those who are worthy. I believe that if I were worthy of understanding I would dream of Annie. This is what I wish before I die: to dream of Annie, if only once and fleetingly.

Vertige Doré

for Anne Waldman and Andrew Schelling

*V*ertige Doré was one of the preeminent scholars of his age and the first to recognize that the archetypal ogress was not the fruit of morbid imaginations, but established in cannibal practice of international significance. What Schliemann did for Troy, proceeding from myth to the unshrouding of a city, Doré did for the ogre and ogress. And he did even more.

His work began in the uncharted regions of Greenland north of Redhook, where, if he lost three fingers to frostbite, he found an aboriginal tribe living as they always had: they were feasting somewhat sadly on human cartilage. His experiences in Redhook are the impulse behind his first major publication, *La Domesticité et l'appetit,* for which Doré received the coveted Niflheim Garter. But Doré outdid himself, surpassing his many rivals when he was able to prove that the Hindu panoply of multilimbed gods was based on a rare yet worldly phenomenon.

Before going any further, let us look briefly into Doré's autobiography, *Memories of an Eccentric Dreamer.* Here the great scholar describes the very things that precipitated him into the fascinations of a lifetime.

"When I gazed upon my mother's willow-patterned dishes, I asked if there were places where the sublime was as constant as air because I wanted above all to travel there. My grandfather, himself an intrepid traveler in his youth and who was now living with us in his decline, his head bent over his bowl, told me that the dust of the Orient smelled unlike the dust at home and described a city in India where elephants were as common as spaniels in France. Although acute antiquity prevented him from lifting his face as he spoke, still I dreamed of strange countries."

Vertige Doré's discovery was greeted with mad laughter. He was thought to be insane, wildly eccentric at best, clearly the victim of an elaborate hoax. De Grave's insipid translations account for his mediocre reception abroad; his masterpiece, *A Race of Gods,* provided belly laughs in the academy when it first appeared. I am certain that disavowed squeamishness, coupled with the nineteenth century's terror of the unique and the monstrous, explains the work's poor reception and the subsequent obscuration of Doré's exemplary find.

But let us return to origins once again, as my readers will be wanting to know—or so I hope—what it is I am talking about. To—as you say in America—*get on with it.* Doré writes:

"Grandfather had given me a small box of Indian sweets, a picture of Malabar Hill painted on one side. The box was green and Malabar Hill was green. Behind it gleamed the Bay of Bengal. I began to dream of a land that smelled of caramel and coconut.

"Soon after," he continues, "when awakening from my afternoon nap earlier than usual, I set out to find some company. It was late summer and as the heat was very intense, everyone was resting in the cool shadows of their shuttered rooms. Surely I was looking for the paternal knee because I found myself standing before Father's study. The door was unlocked and I slipped into a place that inspired a sacred awe.

"Father's desk rose up darkly from the sumptuous Ispahan, and on it, dazzling in the sunlight, lay an open book, the rims of its pages gilded. My curiosity aroused, I climbed onto Father's chair and saw an astonishing, an unforgettable image of Sri Lakshmi, simultaneously emerging from the river Ganges and being showered by two amorous elephants. Her face was immeasurably beautiful, her eyes almond-shaped and black, and her lips smiling. I was captivated by the full orbs of her breasts and her little naked feet. But what seized my imagination above all were her *four arms*. I decided then and there that I would find her. I had not outgrown my belief in fairyland, you see, and so I did not doubt that the miraculous creature was real. My own family seemed insipid ever after, as did my native Provence. I longed for tasseled elephants, lotus blossoms, and the goddess."

By the time Doré took his doctorate in the Eastern religions at the Sorbonne, the Hindu theogony was as familiar to him as the French monarchy. Doré's sister, Valance, was known to tease her brother mercilessly, in public insisting that Vertige would not marry until he had found himself a bride with four arms or more. Doré may have laughed at this along with the rest, but he knew his sister was not far from the truth. He would not be satisfied until he could prove what the inspired intuition of infancy had suggested: that Lakshmi was rooted in the real, that once such a creature had actually walked the earth.

The year was 1857. The Archbishop of Canterbury, having heard of Doré's obsession somehow, wrote begging him to "turn from a heretical Project inspired by Vanity." That same year Doré's own mother, rattling away on her deathbed, ordered her son to desist, and when he refused, disinherited him. Hoping to finance the costly voyage to India with a second publication, Doré completed *The Fairy Pygmies of Ireland*. The volume assured his reputation and it prepared an enthusiastic public for the ultimate revelation that—if it was long in coming—was, after all, well worth waiting for.

Solvent, unfettered by family, Vertige Doré, now thirty-six, booked passage on the *Kashmir Gate*. "A beautiful ship," he wrote Valance, "painted Malabar green." After an uneventful voyage, Doré disembarked at Bombay, "eager to explore the vast Hither and Thither of India," first visiting the place that had engendered all his reveries. Passing toward day's end beneath the Towers of Silence, where the bodies of the dead were beaked to the bone by vultures before crumbling into dust, it occurred to him that every breath he took contained the dust of the dead, and this kept him thoughtful.

"The woods are fat with vultures," he wrote his sister, "but they are also bright with songbirds. And there are so many gardens the air smells not of death but of Paradise." This infatuation with India evolved into a passionate love affair; Doré came to blows with the missionaries who "stuffed their Bibles translated into Hindoostanee and Bengalee* down the throats of their hosts." He did not share their zeal for Christ's bloody hands and feet but instead dreamed of Kali and her blood-filled cup. Perhaps it was the tropical sun, but once when he was introduced to an ambulant minister who had left a translation of Genesis on the altar to Vishnu in Cuddalore, Doré tracked him down in order to slap him once across the face. The art

* Doré's spelling.

historian who likened the sculpted image of the Buddha to "a boiled suet pudding" fared no better.

Attributable to such gestures, Doré obtained favor with the Peishwa of Poona, the last monarch of the Mahrattas, who, when he learned the nature of the scholar's quest, gave him access to his harem because it contained beauties of surprising conformations, and, indeed, Vertige embraced some curious beings there. All had two arms, but one had a lidded fold like a sleeping eye in the middle of her forehead and this spurred him on. Bajee Roo then gave him a guide and his own elephant so that he might explore the obscure regions of the world to find the four-armed beings of his dearest dreams, beings who before chronology, in that time when the things of this world were not considered worth recording, existed in relative profusion.

A eunuch in the Peishwa's custody had told Doré of a monster kept in an alley in a city named Seringapatam, and so he traversed a land rife with missionaries, tigers, lepers, and moaning jackals (as well as soldiers and sepoys—for India was seized by the fever of war) until he came to that city. His disappointment was extreme when after much hardship the creature turned out to be a Siamese twin so thoroughly depraved as to be cruelly deprived of humanity. That night he smoked opium for the first time, losing himself in a weighty weather of numberless dreams.

From there he went to Pooree in the province of Orissa, for he had learned of a village of Holy Jugglers said to have

more arms than other mortals. Because the village was
circumvented by a pit of fire, no one had entered it in over
two hundred years. When the jugglers all proved to have
merely two arms apiece and two hands, and the pit of fire
proved to be an open sewer, he continued on and coura-
geously, too, for that year nearly fourteen hundred had
died poisoned by serpents and close to two thousand eaten
by feral beasts. One hundred languages were spoken in
India then; between them Vertige and his guide were con-
versant in ten.

Late in the year they reached the stone elephants of
Kanârak, and their own elephant—his mild and matronly
face animated by perplexity—stood before these as if
stunned, before kneeling, worshipful—or perhaps attempting to fathom a mystery. "As I gazed at my elephant en-
thralled by the stone statues, I thought that beauty is not a
thing unto itself," Vertige wrote to Valance, "but the vehicle by which the spiritual is revealed." Not long after, they
passed a herd of wild elephants heading east. In the morning they discovered that their own elephant had vanished.

The quest now took on the character of an aesthetic
practice. Doré and his guide—in truth his apprentice—
bathed in sacred rivers, meditated in grottoes, and ate
roots. As they watched, the earth quaked and the sky broke
apart, flooding the land with rain. The sun returned, the
sky closed; clay turned to stone beneath their feet. Months
passed, then years. They took to traveling in a bullock
cart—much as the ancient hierophants of Bihar—with a

woman of unique beauty whom, it is rumored, Vertige engaged for ritual prostitution. It has been said, erroneously perhaps, that Vertige and his mysterious companion fucked in all the temples of Magadha, worshiping as they did the specific moment that was revelatory of all moments, worshiping incandescence, that which "is defined by atmosphere only and revealed by those sublimely, supremely transitory mediums: light, fire, sun, and moon." "Time," Vertige wrote to Valance, "is older than profane history. Sûrya, Uma, and I have now entered into Time. We are one with Time; we *are* Time." There is a rare photograph of the three, Doré sitting with kingly ease beside two beings of incomparable loveliness.

When spring came again they wandered the Valley of Nerbudda on foot. Vertige wrote: "Today I met a fakir worshiping an idol of dung." That night he dreamed that the same fakir appeared to him dressed in a cloak of ashes and he recognized black Kali. Kicking him in the heart so that he fell, she leapt upon his chest and danced there, crushing his ribs into a bloody dust. But he saw her four arms churning like a cosmic windmill and knew he would soon find what he was so desperately looking for.

"Brahma is graced with an infinity of attributes," Doré wrote his sister, "his forms are as mutable as weather. I like to imagine a world in which each creature is mutable, a world in which men might shed their skins, grow wings, awaken with green hair. But the imagination of Brahma is limitless and the next time he engenders a world perhaps sentient beings *will* come in as many colors as the rainbow, grow manes, have violet eyes, claws, fur, and yes—a multitude of arms! A multitude of arms for embracing one another with tenderness.''

That winter Uma perished and Doré's wanderings, always erratic, became more so: he moved like a man insane from place to place as though attempting to travel the ten points of space simultaneously, taking in one season mountains, valleys, cities, lost villages, abandoned palaces, jungle shrines, and desert tombs. For a full decade he wandered thus alone; what happened to his guide Sûrya is not known. Valance believed that her brother was no longer living but a skeleton moldering at the bottom of a well. He was very much alive, however, sleeping in rhododendron glades or among the fragrant cedars of the Himalayan foothills.

Not far from Simla, in a narrow city buried along the mountain flanks, a clear view of Kashmir in the distance, he came upon what he had so diligently sought.

It was November, a night of full moon. Without knowing it he traversed a field where once gentle elephants had been tormented into crushing condemned criminals to death with their feet. Filthy and exhausted, Doré made his way to the river. He bathed, then climbed a hill upon which a temple blazed with candlelight. There a wasted crone approached him with an offer of love in a painted room with a mistress unlike any other, a true *apsarasa*. Since Uma's death Vertige had had no lover, and the old woman's promise awakened a violent longing.

He followed her into a diamond-shaped garden past a number of temples that looked like the mountains of some ideal planet of the mind. India had never ceased to astonish him, and even now he felt he navigated a hallucination. Peering into the portals as he passed, he saw that the temple walls were fissured, pitted, and green yet beautiful still, animated by scenes of amorous intention and fulfillment, scenes of coupling as infinite as the stars, entire zodiacs of love. The very air he breathed sparked with sexual tension so that when at last he entered the place of assignation, the promise of rare delight had taken possession of his soul.

Although Vertige Doré had witnessed many splendors in India—pools brimming with iris the color of the sky, forests milling with deer, the Trimurti dancing in a room of lapis lazuli, infants nursed by sagacious elephants—nothing had prepared him, and this despite a lifetime of dreaming, for what he was about to see.

They entered a temple so ancient it appeared to pulse beneath a weight of trees and plants. Having insinuated themselves into a corridor that, clotted with earth and roots, spiraled into the temple's heart, they came to a polychromatic room open to the sky and bathed in moonlight. Here the crone vanished, leaving Doré standing alone before a fountain that was churning with such savage energy water became milk and milk fire and fire a violently animated air. As he stood marveling at this impossibility—a fountain of milk that was also a wind and a fire—a radiance filled his mind like the opening of a third eye and Doré saw his father's study and the images he had admired as a child, cataclysms for the most part—floods, volcanic eruptions, a tower toppled by an earthquake, a ship by a storm, and solar eclipses, and the cool, beneficial moon, the sweep of the stars: some were planets forming and flourishing and pulsing. And he saw these things were drops of rain scattered upon the coiling, the uncoiling body of time. As Doré wrote to Valance:

"Then—and how strange it was!—one of these worlds became increasingly distinct. As the others receded, it revealed itself to be the box of sweets Grandfather had given me so many years before, Malabar Hill painted on one side.

"As I gazed upon the spinning box I was seized by eager expectancy. For I knew that the box, now glowing eerily, did not contain caramels but something of significance.

"And now the picture of Malabar Hill was no longer still but an animated space, a living world, and I—precipitated by some visionary mechanism—was at its threshold, already entering into the weather of another time, another place: the time and place of all my longings. When my feet touched ground, I moved among the people of my dreams.

"At the entrance to a market, a woman—her laughter lighter than air—offered me fruit with each of her four hands. An instant later, behind a stall of flowers, a baby, like a starfish, spilled from its mother's womb and reached for its mother's face. Lovers embraced. I saw exemplary cobblers and weavers, milkmaids and temple dancers; saw a unique harvest and the nimblest of four-armed sailors.

"And then I saw this astonishing people hunted down as the sound of war filled the air with its foul thunder. I saw harvests of blood, saw infants sucking stones, children eating clay. I saw the bones of an entire people turn to dust and in the wind, scatter. I saw Malabar Hill on fire. And the room in which I stood appeared to catch fire.

"Then, as I looked, the vortex of images stilled, a deeper, brighter eye opened in my mind and my soul blossomed anew with an intuition like the approach of ecstasy. Emerging from the churning fire, turning slowly in a silk sari the color of water, was a woman as fugitive as wind, as refreshing as water. And I was dissolving into the infinity of her embrace. She, too, had four arms. Above us the moon and stars rose and fell with equal velocity."

Over the next number of years, Vertige Doré vanished once again. His travels had taken on a renewed purpose. The beautiful aberration in the ancient room was the first indication of an itinerary that—as he moved from one like phenomenon to another—extended across India in a web of temple brothels and sacred rooms. Winning the trust and the love of these marvelous beings, Vertige Doré was able to trace family trees going back many centuries, genetic events as undeniable, as significant, as black skin, white skin, green eyes, red hair.

When Vertige Doré's name resurged, it was in conjunction with a strange and compelling book—the book that is the object of this essay. Concerned lest these beings he loved be harmed by murderous zealots, puritans, and fools, the book contains no maps, no specific designations. But it is rich in stunning photographs too vivid to be denied, as are the compelling stories of beings, told with grace and sweetness—beings exactly like us in all ways but one.

Of her brother, Valance was to say by way of a eulogy:

"He was a philosopher. By that I mean he was fearless, eager to enter abysses both real and imagined; eager to explore the unexplored and the unimagined. And by philosopher I mean he was also wanting to do battle with those things that frightened him the most. He called them the Enigmas: Enigmas of Mind. For example, he never ceased to wonder at the evil he saw everywhere, man's seemingly infinite capacity to do harm.

"My brother dared enter the planet's most secret places. He returned with the promise of transcendence. What Vertige Doré offered us, in the form of uniquely constituted beings, was another chance to accept the world's diversity—diversity not as a proof of chaos, but of munificence, not as a curse, *but as a gift.*"

The Many Tenses of Wanting

for Jonathan

Doctor—

I have come to you with the expectation that together we will sever the knot of my perplexed (my perpetual!) infancy.

Weighted down by virtual baggage, I am not—as you noted instantly—an autonomous being, and autonomy is precisely what I am wanting. However, I have what you call a sexual soul, or rather, the capacity to evolve into a sexual being, to reveal an authentic blue streak, the capacity not only to inspire but to withstand heat, to weather my stripes and to shed my old skin. I intend to astonish us both.

You asked me any number of things; you startled me. Almost at once my heart quickened with something like hope: Is he really after the truth? Is he able to look into the darkest corners of the heart without flinching? The man is no prude, I thought, and furthermore he is smart. And good-looking. Sumerian! A Semitic face, the beard threaded with silver, nose prominent, eyes deepest black. Not that I—supine on the little couch and staring at the ceiling in the classic pose—got to see much of your face!

Again: You asked me any number of things—all interesting and necessary, and this *despite the risks* you described, or, as you so engagingly revealed to me—*because of the risks implied*. Obviously, as you pointed out, there is always danger when the engagement is acute. As in passionate loving. "We are talking about real life here," you said; "that is the intention of the work we have undertaken together."

A thrilling phrase! I think of Houdini unpuzzling his chains and rising to the surface of his man-size aquarium. *Undertaken together!* I shall help you rob my own grave so that I may steal away with my own intrinsic capacity *to be someone*. It occurs to me that to engage in the world of the living one *must be prompt*. If only because there is so little time. (And yet there you sit, Doctor, graying at the temples. Don't you hear the winds of time raging about your little office in the sky?)

I have always been sluggish. Although my infancy was punctuated by my mother's rallying cry, "Step on it!" I misunderstood. I thought that time was to be killed, crushed beneath the foot like a centipede else it leap to my leg and inflict a mortal sting. I imagined wasting away. You evoked Plotinus and Jung simultaneously when you added: "Each memory, dream, and reflection must inform the immediate present. We are," you said also, "about to confront the chaos of cryptic language. But rest assured: the characters, runes, wedges, hieroglyphs, whatever—all mean something." And so: the vortex I carry within me, just as chaos itself, is simply an undeciphered, an uncharted system.

∽

My first memories are of such uncharted and undeciphered spaces, of a white light which was the sky over Iran, a brilliant light illuminating particles of dust. I was, perhaps, three or four and had no notion of numbers but surely a sense of the infinite because I recall that sky and those reeling particles with an extreme fear as though I could be swallowed up in such a swarming. The world revealed itself to me at that moment and for the first time. My senses were accosted on all sides at once and so great was that swarm in my mind that to this day I believe I saw a man with the head of a camel and a donkey with a man's body and as alive as you and I.

My father was president of both the American Bible Society and a soft drink company; he hoped to convince his Iranian hosts of the inevitability of Christ and carbonated coffee. He failed, but even now the short years we spent in Iran animate my dreams. For example, I have a recurrent dream of a bazaar in which upon the unpaved

dirt all things of significance are laid out—not only dates
and sugarcane but ideas: the idea of color and the idea of
music; flavors, also, the gummy eyes of children going
blind, luxurious grief and violent anger, passionate love
and wickedness, fragments of poetry, the Supreme Deity
(and he is a cherub with the body of a bull and the head of
a man), the Fall of Man, the cattle of the field, the pine
tree of Eridu, the severed head of our servant—his name
was Hadji—Hadji's head displayed like a geographer's plaster model, his ruined eye a volcano, the scar (from temple
to chin) a river of fire. Although it was not Hadji's head
that was cut off but his hand—for he had stolen a box of
Bisquick from my mother's kitchen. My father attempted
to beg for leniency, but by preparing American pancakes
for his family in his hovel, Hadji had dishonored his country. So that the final months in Iran were marked by shame
and horror and all the ensuing hocus-pocus; my parents,
motivated by dread, argued the Bible's most cryptic pas-
sages and then Mother fled the ancient world for the new
in a fit of loathing (and she took me with her).

Another early memory (and this before I was to learn of
Hadji's downfall) is of a visit to the vanished Tower of
Babel in a heat so intense I was stricken with fever and
nearly died; the little cotton kerchief my mother had tied
about my head doing nothing to protect me from the furi-
ous eye of the sun. And—is it surprising?—for days I spoke
in a confusion of tongues. I sounded like a Finn speaking
about Babylonian legal codes in Turkish was my mother's

joke. My mother was a wit—far too smart for Father, whose mind plodded at best. But even though we left Iran when I was not yet nine, I still believe, deep in my soul, that the stars, the moon, and the sun rule over our days and nights. I mean I cannot look at them without shuddering as though they were so many feral creatures threatening to sever my limbs with one bite should I fail to pay attention, fail to be on time. I'm always in a panic I'll miss something essential. For example, I noticed your habit of caressing your lower lip with the knuckle of your left index finger— a charming gesture, seductive, actually (and this is why I recall the things you said so clearly). And I think there may be a key here—some sort of explanation as to why I am so *consummately Babylonian* in my neurotic comportment—I am making reference here to my habits—*obsessions* if you will: there are days when I dare not remove my clothes, or wear white, or speak in public, or take medicine, or utter a curse. This is why I have come to you. It has become increasingly difficult for me to function in the world. Last week I was unable to utter a word; I was afraid of being sexually penetrated by moonlight, by the volatile essences of plants and the vapor of the bath.

I was told that you are "a man of spirit" and I have not been disappointed. Our first meeting was, to my mind, exceptional. Until now my therapists have all been hand-holders, potential thugs, or mystics. You will not attempt to bludgeon me with terminology, demand that I worship in the Holy Temple of Freud, look for the goddess within, mother me, seduce me—*or allow me to seduce you*—for, as you noted, I am a pretty woman, youthful for my age and due to my diminutive size and Oriental features (my mother was Japanese) doll-like, even—a thing that endears me to older men.

And because I am somehow *intact* (and now we come to the heart of the matter), having—in the sexual act—always managed *to be elsewhere,* I fascinate many men (and women too); they pride themselves in this way: they think they will be the one to awaken me. But no one has. I may spend hours altogether gazing at images of lust, for example the Babylonian figures of Enkidu and the whore copulating shamelessly, limbs spread, tense, contorted, in collision like forces of nature. . . . Or I read the little sonnets of the Renaissance: *Open your thighs so I can look straight at your beautiful* culo *and* potta *before my face* and so on—without being aroused. In fact, it is a game I play with myself, to look upon these things with disinterest, coolly, as one might examine the sexual encounters of fish. And yet I am certain that it could be otherwise and wish it were so, for my loneliness is intolerable and I fear I shall become a hag of ice—if I am not that already.

To continue: I am assured having met with you once that between the two of us—despite a powerful attraction on my part—because yes, I am capable of feeling attraction and relish the chase (an attraction that has more to do with affinities than transference—it is far too soon to speak of transference!)—there will be no foolishness! You will not step across the Kilim that separates us like a sea to embrace me. I will not hear you whisper: *Open your thighs so I can look straight at your beautiful* culo *and* potta *before my face.* I will not see ardor in your eyes, nor will you in mine. More's the pity. We will engage in matters of the spirit, only. Despite the affinities that clearly exist (after an hour, only! An hour!) between our bodies and our souls. (For it is possible—and the irony here is unbearable—that you—in other circumstances—could be the one to awaken me. How sweet it would be to long for you!) But there will be no lovemaking. Your rigor in such matters is exemplary. Your high social character. Your sound judgment and moral worth. Your marriage, the children of college age—I have done my own investigating—all this has decided me to come to you. After so many failures. Yes. You will give me a *sexual soul*—as you put it—but not by fucking me. Although, as I have said, so many find me irresistible. And this because I am the bright mirror of desire; I am like a clay that is never touched by fire and so may be modeled again and again. (This said, I bruise easily. A lover once left parallel thumbprints on the inside of both my knees and beneath each buttock. My skin so white, the marks blue—a strange tattoo. How beautiful I looked after! How mysterious! I crawled up on the bathroom sink, my buttocks to the glass, and gazed at those two marks, at my ass, my cunt beneath, imagining that I was my own lover. *Open your thighs so I* . . . Any other woman would have been dizzied by the sight!)

∽

Even in my infancy I was beautiful. In Babylon, Hadji proposed daily that I should be rolled in powdered sugar and eaten with a spoon. Once when we traveled *en famille* in a gufa—so like a wooden bowl floating in the water—his conceit seemed so apt it terrified me. I was in the bowl—where was Hadji's spoon?

Hadji told great stories. My favorite was about the caliph al-Mamoon who showered his bride with pearls. Living in a household rigorous in the denial of luxury and pleasure, how could the story not impress me? Ever since Hadji and my time in Babylon, sugar is not sweet enough, nor red red enough. No man will spill pearls on *my* head! Although I expect your words, Doctor, will be that precious, that illuminating. You see—I expect wonders of another sort from you, from us; yes: our minds will catch fire. My eternal winter will quicken into spring and I shall know summer and I shall know what it is to live in the world, to live in a body.

After Hadji lost his hand and we prepared to depart from Iran, Father projected a voyage to distant lands even beyond Ethiopia. He explained that the people living there were without lineage and had no knowledge of the Flood. A people without knowledge of the Flood! A people like a clean, soft clay upon whom he could impress his idea of the divine. He would tame them with the fear of Jehovah and civilize them with coffee cola. He would set a holy fire beneath their seats and precipitate them into industrious bees in a hive of his own making.

Imagine! Heathens dressed in overalls reciting the Lord's Prayer while drinking soda pop—while *producing* soda pop! He would be the Henry Ford of Nubia! He would precipitate an entire race into history. He would introduce them to the Flood: the ebb and tide of capital! Already imagining his advertising campaign—*The only cola made with God's own rain!*—he imagined cisterns, fields of cane sugar, and hillsides green with Ethiopian coffee. Mother was silent. She knew Nubia was as arid as her own life.

You can tell that Father was not much of a reader— apart from the Bible, his accounting books, his well-thumbed copy of Burkitt's *Climate, Costs, and Coffee.* What he knew about the world he had learned in Sunday school. Often he was irked by what he called Mother's *Japanese queerness.* (You are wondering how they met: at a church supper in Flushing, New York.) Mother now said: "Cola has failed in Mesopotamia. Why should it flourish in Nubia?" Father replied: "A question of faith." He had figured it all out, you see: God had purposely made the business fail, had even tempted Hadji's greed "so that we should move on"—a remark that put my mother irremediably out of patience. She said: "I don't think God gives a fig for soda pop, or a fig for Nubians either, for that matter." And she had refused to follow him. The last we heard he had entered a bugless land of blasted rock that stretched toward infinity beneath a sapphire blue sky. Like a man from an earlier age, Father had set off with a case of Bibles. At some point he bought a rug and managed to post it. I still have it—a rug woven by the people for whom it is heresy to portray anything recognizable. Yet in those strenuous geometries I can see figures hiding and it seems to me that they are sexual, that the rug is a species of star chart of erotic associations. I am certain that had Father *looked* at the rug he would not have bought it. After that we never heard from him again.

We were living in Manhattan. Mother had two ribs removed and became an exotic dancer with a very small waist. Once she awakened wildly laughing, having dreamed Father was a centipede beetling his way across an infinity of rubble bringing Bibles to people who worshiped anthills. Before she died—having made a name for herself in that curious milieu she had chosen (there's a portrait of her by Pinsky in the Hines)—she told me: "Your father was the biggest bore and the greatest fool I ever knew."

And she dreamed of Hadji—a nightmare I share (and I don't know who dreamed it first)—of Hadji's hand rigid in the sky—horizontal—rather like an oddly shaped dirigible—pointing toward a black cloud (Father's black Africa) and Father's certain death. "A man who dreamed of soda pop," Mother said, "and who probably died of thirst." Poor Father. A zealot and a hayseed with imperialist dreams. "He was like coffee cola," Mother said; "an undrinkable mixture."

⸜⸝

I believe it is so that one's sexuality is fixed at an early age. One is impressionable and a visual experience has the impress of a firebrand. I mean one can see something so puissant it sets the mind on fire, an inextinguishable fire that—if it cools to embers with the passage of hours and days—can be rekindled by a random word.

One day in Babylon, Hadji proposed a tour of the restricted quarters of the city. Mother took to the idea and suggested we disguise ourselves. She was a creature who loved a good joke and good time—as life without Father would reveal—and she sent Hadji to fetch some clothes for the two of us. I wore one of Hadji's shirts—it fell to my ankles (for Hadji was a broad, a robust man)—and put my beach sandals on; to assure the effect, Mother cut my hair. A tomboy, I was delighted to see all my curls gathering in a heap on the floor, although Hadji, distressed by the amplitude of my mother's enthusiasm, mournfully cried: *"Pity! Pity!"* with each snip of scissors. Seeing that he looked at the hair with longing as well as regret, Mother bent down and retrieved one curl. I laughed when he put it to his lips and kissed it, laughed to feel my naked neck in the morning breeze, to see myself transformed into an Arab boy. In Hadji's long coat, turban, and scarves, Mother looked positively *calif.*

Doctor. Not a night passes without my dreaming of that morning. I dream of fractured cobbled paths, of palaces leaning over the street, and sudden courtyards. Free of Father for the day and feeling festive, we tasted everything: cakes as yellow as pollen, preserved apricots, buffalo cream thick and sweetened with Syrian honey.

"Now you are truly seeing my country," Hadji exclaimed, and Mother said (and I had never seen her so happy) "I *love* your country!" She bit into an apricot and honey spilled down her chin. And I, intoxicated by her buoyancy, by the mysteries offered everywhere I looked, ran off into an *impasse* hung with wet silk; I ran until I came to an elaborately carved gate. I recognized honeysuckle vines and fruits—the "sacred tree" of the Assyrians. Through the interstices of the vines I could discern a courtyard of blue and turquoise tiles shining from a recent washing. Beyond the courtyard was an open door and on the threshold stood a beautiful woman, her robe open to reveal the deep cleft of her breasts, her nipples stained red, the black moss of her pubic hair. Her eyes were so black they seemed to shadow her face. She was smoking and daydreaming and did not see me. As she lifted the cigarette to her lips I saw that her hands, too, were stained red. But then Hadji was beside me, pulling me away from the gate, then lifting me into his arms as he whispered: "Forbidden! Forbidden!" Just as he turned with me to flee from that marvelous place, I saw a painting on the wall beside the gate of an erect phallus animated by wings, a rooster-phallus ejaculating sperm in the shape of leaves and flowers.

Although I was only a slip of a girl at the time—little more than seven—I grasped what I had seen and was astonished by it. I had seen Bathsheba, I knew; I had seen through the gate of Sodom; I had seen the phallus Father had tried so hard to deny. It was the phallus a schoolmate had once drawn on the blackboard with chalk, the phallus of the winged gods of Mesopotamia.

As we burst from the alley and returned to the street where Mother was waiting gorging on fruit, I felt something thrash wildly against my ribs. It was Hadji's cock, and it startled us both. At once he set me down on my feet as I looked to his body and the place where I knew I must see something of the powerful form I had felt leaping against me. Hadji pulled his robes about him and, pretending that nothing out of the ordinary had happened, proposed lunch. He took us to a diminutive restaurant painted with birds and lions; an antique room—the paintings were faded and pocked, and this made them all the more wonderful. I felt that we had somehow entered into the sacred precincts beyond the gate, as though the forbidden space could not be circumvented because it exerted an influence upon the entire city: it was the place of the world's heartbeat and all paths led there.

Hadji ordered the best and insisted that we were his guests—although the meal must have cost him a full week's

salary. Barley loaves and roasted chickens stuffed with al-
monds and grilled seeds, the cow's first milk after the calf is
born, slices of hard white honey. But rather than dispel the
vision and the touch of Eros on fire, the feast heightened
my impressions so that the forbidden moments continued
to burn in my mind. The near-naked body of the mysterious whore and the body of the man Hadji took on the
savors and fragrances of fruit and milk and honey. The
Whore in the Courtyard, the Whore of the Full Breasts
and Black Triangle—she became the image of the woman
I would become, aflame in the bright light of late morning.

Doctor—can you see how that morning the incombus-
tible palace of sex had been revealed too me in all its sumptuous mystery? Is it a wonder, Beloved Friend, that red is
no longer red enough? That sugar is not sweet enough?
My laughter only a seeming? How could any encounter
re-create the splendor of that morning, the astonishment,
the heat, the fresh knowledge of those instants?

I have taken the thrashing phallus into my mouth and
tasted it blossoming there. I have taken the winged phallus
into my entrails, where it has reared its head and probed for
my heart. Yet I remain to be awakened, for nothing has
thus far given back the promise of that fated morning, that
terrible morning when as we left the painted room Hadji
was seized, and shouting taken from us. Because a jealous
neighbor had seen the strange cakes on the plate—made
just as Mother had shown Hadji how to make them.

Father had been questioned in his office—had the flour, the can of Danish butter, the maple syrup been gifts? Father was shocked. Hadji had stolen—that much was clear. The devil had tempted his hand. A week passed. Mother insisted that Father intervene; Hadji's wife had come to our door, weeping. That night Father described the bandaged stump that Hadji, alone in his little cell, grieved over, holding it delicately with his left hand.

"I told him to trust in God," Father said. "And he looked at me strangely. I think he is angry with me although what happened is clearly not my fault. After all, I told them to be compassionate." Hadji, Father decided, was unlucky. But he was a thief and to have lied to the authorities to save him was unthinkable. "One does not sin for a sinner. They're all thieves," Father decided. And he began to dream of an untouched people of clay.

I, too, dreamed of clay. As Mother and I sailed to New York City I dreamed of a clay body: malleable and insensible. Sailing a sea of lead beneath a leaden sky I thought: The one safe place is the space of an instant, an instant seized forever in a tableau of fire and ice: a fixed picture of a woman ungraspable, perceived as she dreams. And her dreams take her far, far away from the world, its terrors and losses.

∽

Doctor, now you have it all: the enchanted island lost to sight, the voyage ever after ghostly and stark. You will say that my "all" is only the point of departure, that the voyage we have undertaken has only just begun. To tell the truth I am wild with expectation. Will you, I wonder, as tall, as broad as Hadji and despite the dangers, have the courage to give me back the fullness of that primal vision?

By the time you get this letter I will be making my way to your little anteroom, where I will sit killing time with a magazine. I wonder: Will you have the courage to look me in the eyes? Will you find the words? Will words be necessary?

Think of it: I am virtually that perfect creature of an Arabian night's dream. Once you have opened the gate will you be able to resist me? Would that be wise? For—and of this I am certain—together we will transcend the entire process of recovery. By the time it is over and we have given Hadji back his hand and me my heart, we will be like the first man and the first woman lying naked together; you will lean into me the way the storm leans into the trees.

The Student from Algiers

The war has been over for only a few months, and because the French have left countless mines scattered throughout the Aurès, she cannot leave the jeep and wander, although there are many points of interest along the way, including the abandoned village of Zaouia, where she had lived, briefly, before the war. Passing near Zaouia she can see the mosque, its walls deeply scarred by machine-gun fire, its ruined minaret blackened by smoke. Zaouia where she had learned to crack melon seeds with her teeth.

That night she lies on Djamila's roof gazing at the constellations: Iouemen—"the Little Gazelles"; Chet Edoth—"the Night Maidens"; Talemt—"the She-camel." The sky moves around her like a great mouth; she is held in the

mouth of the sky and expects to be swallowed whole.
Later, when Djamila brings her a blanket, the two women
gaze up at the sky together, talking long into the night.
She tells how when in Zaouia, she had taken a lover, a
student from Algiers on his way to the M'zab. She had said
to him laughing, the first time they kissed: "I want you to
swallow me whole!" And he, his English good, if somewhat stiff, had said: "I shall swallow you whole, but also,
please, in parts."

Hearing this, Djamila roars with laughter, precipitating
a shower of stars. "You Yankee!" she cries with delight, "I
cannot believe you talk this way to men!" "Not any man,"
she says. "The one in Zaouia. The entire affair was marked
by this playfulness." "Our men are not playful." Djamila is
perplexed. "This man of yours, this student from Algiers,
was a pearl in a sea of sand."

Before coming to Algeria she had been warned that the
Algerians were haughty, stern, "madly severe." But despite
the rigors and terrors of the war, her experience proves
otherwise. Even perfect strangers are affable, generous. She
finds a gentle kindness everywhere, a tender curiosity.
Above all: a powerful sense of renewal. The war is over, the
dead counted and mourned; lands are being reforested and
children have returned to school. Her old friend, Djamila,
has planted barley, lentils, melons, and onions; a small
orchard. At dawn she awakens to the sound of turtledoves,

and, moments later, when she strolls along the Wed Biskra with Djamila, they see a flock of wild ducks billing the shallow waters.

The morning he had left Zaouia, the student from Algiers said to her: "You must live in Algeria with the imagination of the dreamer." She had wanted him to say: "Come with me." Or even: "I will return to you." But he did not. She had supposed there was a woman waiting in Algiers—dark, long-boned, irreplaceable. How beautiful were the unveiled women of Algiers! Then, in the weeks and months after his departure she had lived a dream of such wanting that when Hugo had joined her group at the diggings near Erg Tekchouli, he had appeared to her like an oasis hazy with the promise of water.

The night she had accepted Hugo, and as she slept beside him, she dreamed that she was walking naked and alone down the corridors of a dark hotel. Suddenly the student from Algiers was standing before her, gazing at her with scorn. Points of fire, his eyes burned her body with the terrible, the precise heat of an incandescent cigarette. She awakened in a place she did not recognize, nor did she recognize the man beside her, the one she had chosen, the one she did not love.

Illumined by a thin blade of moonlight, a white scorpion was climbing the wall. She was in her own tent somewhere off the camel *piste* to In Salah. In the dark Hugo seemed far too large to be human. He lay beside her like a thing of necromantic clay she had conjured from weakness or folly. And yet a few hours earlier, Hugo had covered her body with kisses and held her naked feet in his hands. What had she been thinking of? But then, as if to prove she was in love and madly, she pressed against him, murmuring his name. Had the student from Algiers been standing in the shadows, he would have been fooled.

This morning on her way to the M'zab, her humiliation and rage are such she is tempted to tear her hair, tear the flesh of her face and neck as she has seen the women of the desert do in times of acute distress. Her injured, ill-used heart is become so wasted as to cause her constant pain— the dull ache of sorrow and something like dread. Because she has come to understand that if the student from Algiers never told her his name, had left without an address or a word, it is because he was somehow actively engaged in the insurrection which, during her time in Zaouia, had evolved into a full-scale revolutionary war.

Could she rip into her chest now and pull her heart out by the roots it would not be recognizable. She describes her heart to herself as she muses over a scarlet land that, in the morning sun, appears to bleed: a tiny shell, a dead shell black as soot, heavy as gravity, and pumping a dirty water.

Here in the Sahara she can become a perfume, a melody, pure thought. She can become an erasure, silence. Yes, she can become an absence, the air in suspension between two grains of sand. All this as a way out, as a way of excising the humiliation of having chosen Hugo. As a way of excising the terrible, the imperious longing for the one in Zaouia who had vanished so suddenly she had spent the next set of days standing in a sand-laden wind, watching the land weather away.

Now on her way south, the sun spills over the road like a hot tide and the red desert metamorphoses into a mirror reflection of a blond sky, transparent, almost ethereal. How she loves this mutable land, the hours spent puzzling over the fragments of a vanished world, fragments of an insufficient alphabet: ostrich-shell beads, implements of quartzitic sandstone, of clear chalcedony, moss agate, fine jasper. Red and yellow ochre. Ivory needles and combs. Shells charred by fire. Things she takes pleasure in recording in pencil or ink on large sheets of heavy paper.

Before the war, at a site near Erg Tekchouli, she had found a pearl, the largest she had ever seen and the most beautifully worked. A week later, visiting a Tuareg encampment, she saw virtually the same bead hanging from the lovely neck of a living girl. With gravity the girl had offered her a bowl of milk and all at once the dust of the excavations had become a measurement of the real. Ever after when she found a bead of ostrich shell or a glass pearl, she saw the girl's intent face and tasted milk.

The projects she and Hugo worked on together were sponsored by the museum of a prestigious American university. But it seemed to her that the artifacts they found belonged to the desert, not to them. That having documented the sites they should return everything. Hugo pointed out that the university paid them for more than

knowledge; the university wanted artifacts, and her senti-
mentalism would cost them both a job. She fell silent but
continued brooding: *Every single thing we find is a potency,
has meaning.* The glass pearl the girl wore was blue—the
inimitable blue of Heaven; was white—the white of the
molar of the healthy servant girl; was gray—the color of
the turtledove, of constancy.

For a few months there was another woman involved in
the project—Monica, so blond, so pale she had a tendency
to vanish like a lizard in the sand. Early on Hugo began to
implore her, whenever he made love to her, to seduce
Monica, to bring her into their bed. She refused, not because she loved him but, perhaps, because she did not love
him enough. (Although she supposed that had she loved
him enough, the thought of sharing him would have been
unbearable; the thought of watching him enter the body of
another, unbearable; unbearable too, Monica's eyes watching them.) Monica, flamboyant, a healthy animal, her body
the color of sand, deserved better.

When she thinks of Hugo, she feels ashamed for him
and for herself. What is it the French say? *Hélas, Hélas!*
And the Arabs? *Ya! Allah!* (The times, she knows, were
humiliating for them all.) This morning as she left Biskra,
Djamila had said: "It is time for us all to shed our skins."
Djamila was referring to a man lost to the war.

After the museum project was canceled she returned to America with Hugo because by then she feared that if she left him he would die. She began to think of herself as Hugo's "keeper" as though he were a beast—and this even after she was well aware that he lived in a cage of his own making. But then one morning she awoke with the thought: *I have been skinned alive.* And: *I have allowed myself to be peeled, peeled and eaten like a piece of fruit.* At least she had recognized that Hugo was her cage, the cage of her own taking. She was the one kept.

Eaten like a piece of fruit. The sensuality of this image sends her thoughts winging back to the student from Algiers. Her love for him is like a continuous water, a true desert where everything glistens. One by one she recalls their nights of red clay, their red nights, those generous nights when endearments murmured unceasingly like water.

She ponders this: When the student from Algiers had taken her flesh in his mouth, he had healed her of a wound she had not known she had. The night she had taken Hugo into her tent, that wound had reopened.

She is now approaching the white cliffs and green palms of Berriane, an oasis of the M'zab. A golden eagle accompanies her; flying high he shines in the late afternoon sun like molten metal. Somewhere in the M'zab she hopes to find her lover's traces. She sees the eagle as an auspicious sign.

❦

Each morning in Berriane, Belaid brings her a bowl of fresh camel milk and a wheel of unleavened bread. He brings her a basket of dates, pomegranates, figs. Sometimes he brings her *tikomaren*—the dried cheese of the Tuaregs of the Ahaggar—because she told him how, before the war on her travels in that region, she had come to love it— "like gnawing stones!" "And glass!" Belaid had laughed. "You need a gizzard to digest in the desert!"

She pays him every day, the coins sewn to a piece of heavy drawing paper, beneath a sketch of the palms or a clump of tamarisks, the distant mountains, the ravine. Or a portrait, or the palms swarming with turtledoves, or children harvesting quinces. This time her project is a book, the visions of a dreamer, the dreamer of the Sahara she has become. She wants to capture it all, to capture the shape of time, to offer it lovingly to the one who has vanished, one for whom love had been a living water.

Today when Belaid comes she is sweeping sand from the guesthouse rooms and from the little courtyard where they will drink tea together and delight in one another's conversation. In his youth, Belaid had been an itinerant singer and now if his voice is broken, still he has not lost his gifts entirely. A handsome man, close to eighty, he has already confided, not without pride, that as he had "floated" from the M'zab to the Ahaggar, he had fathered minstrels, magicians, acrobats, a skilled weaver, and warriors: two of his sons had gone north to fight the French in the Aurès.

Knowing how well the women of the Sahara are watched, she had expressed surprise. "Entertainers are like fish in water," Belaid explained. "We winnow our way into this and that." Clapping his hands he burst into song:

> *The Sahara is a Palace of Trespass,*
> *The gate to a world where nothing is fixed,*
> *Where everything scatters like swallows and swifts,*
> *Where everything scatters like sand.*
> *Life flows through the fingers like water;*
> *Love bruises the fingers like sand.*

Belaid learned to speak the dialects of the women he loved, the children he fathered: *zenaga, hassania, tamachek, azeir* . . . a precious capacity he offered to the FLN when news of the insurrection had reached Berriane. "I, my sons, and my daughters spun a web of words," he told her, "from Biskra to Tassili." He continued: "I could never carry a gun, but in my way I fought the French, the same French who, when I was a little boy, measured the heads of everyone in Berriane, even the heads of the women: my mother's and sisters' and aunts'. They fingered us like insects, like rotten fruit. Those fingers left a mark at my temple, here—" He had turned his head to show her a small, red mole. "After they left we scrubbed our bodies with stones. My mother said: 'In the entire universe there is not enough water to wash away the shame.' This I will never forget."

Later, when a French soldier cut the breasts from a girl who had been caught taking water to the rebels, Belaid was not surprised. And when the villagers of Zaouia were lined up against the wall of the mosque, "lined up like empty bottles and shot," no, he had not been surprised. And when the *paras* had brought out the *gígène* and pushed a live wire into his most private place, he had not been surprised and he had not talked, either.

Belaid is now before her, smiling what can only be called a complicitous smile. And this because they have shared so much sadness, so much laughter this past week, told one another so many stories. He bows his head and lifts his hands briefly in greeting:

"Le salut sur vous!"

"Sur vous le salut!"

Today he has brought her gifts: a lettuce from his own garden and freshly fried fritters to go with their morning tea. His granddaughter has made the fritters. It is nine o'clock. Together they will eat the fritters and talk. Perhaps they will talk for so long they will get hungry again and she will get up to fetch dates from the kitchen, and milk. They will sit in the shade of the ancient tamarisk on a palm mat so clean a baby could be born there, and Belaid will sing and they will exchange the stories of their lives,

which, now that they have begun to tell them, could prove
to be without end.

∾

Belaid will never allow her to make the tea. He has his
own eccentric English teapot he keeps polished to a high
shine and carries about in a box. The guesthouse's little
kerosene stove is shining brightly too. When he sees it
Belaid cries: "There is little to occupy you here!" "Baba!"
she scolds him. "You've seen my drawings! You know how
busy I am!" "Yes, I do know. Beautiful drawings. You are
an artist, you—the unveiled American woman who draws
Algerian pictures with Italian pencils on French paper and
who goes about dressed in pantaloons—"

"I offend you!"

"No! Not at all. I am a free thinker. There are not many
free thinkers here."

"Nor where I come from."

"But, I am wondering . . ."

"Yes? I give you permission, Baba, to wonder out
loud."

"Why she is alone, the lady in pantaloons. She is too
pretty to be alone—you will excuse an old man for speaking the truth. Again and again I ask myself: *Why is she not
married?*"

"Because I am divorced." Suddenly giddy she adds,
laughing: "Three times I said: 'I divorce thee.'"

"Is this possible? Such a thing!" Belaid widens his eyes in mock astonishment. "Allah be praised," he says, "that American women can divorce so easily, like Tuaregs."

"But *I am* a Tuareg! Baba—you've seen me on a camel. You've seen me eat *tikomaren* and *kessra!*"

He roars with laughter:

"The Tuaregs may know how to divorce, but they don't know how to eat!"

"Those who know how to divorce know how to eat!"

"You are a fast talker," he complains, or pretends to. "Put a woman in pantaloons and she'll talk off a man's ears!" Belaid begins to sing:

> *I knew such a one in Metlili*
> *Who lost both his ears in this manner.*
> *His wife bit off his nose next*
> *And tied up his tongue—*
> *He's as smooth as an egg, now*
> *And a stammerer.*

"Baba," she says, "I truly wish you were several decades younger."

"Ya! Allah!" He pours her a second cup of tea. *"Hélas, hélas, jolie dame."*

Burning hot the tea is her only luxury and it warms her to the marrow. The tea, the friendship with Belaid, his stories, the songs he sings in a voice that seems to have been hammered out of a thin sheet of brass. An ancient voice that bent by time has traces of verdigris pocking its bright surface.

The landscape, too, is a luxury. Its silence is wonderful, the tangible proof that when Allah made the world he paused between two spoken words. And what if Allah had spoken too quickly? Would those words have collided causing a conflagration? As it was the pause was almost too brief. During the middle of the day it is so hot nothing moves. This is when she chooses the coolest room in the guesthouse, tiled and dark, to sit as still as a stone, her mind suspended in her skull like the egg of a bird that hatches only after a thousand years' incubation. Her mind a stone at the bottom of a deep pool, her thoughts water.

"What are you thinking? You are very far away!"

"I am thinking I want to hear you sing again, Baba, even though—pardon me telling an old man the truth—your voice is like a brass tray pelted with sand."

"Ah, I am fortunate to sing at all. I am fortunate the French did not force me to swallow the wire as they did my friend Abdelaziz. When he cried out, 'Pity! Pity for God's sake!' the *paras* replied: 'No pity for Arabs.' "

She fears she has hurt him and lowers her eyes. For a time they sip their tea in silence. But then Belaid begins to sing. He sings a wordless melody that gently fingers her heart, a thrilling melody that causes her to close her eyes in rapture. Almost before she is aware of it the words are winging, words in classical Arabic, very unlike Belaid's own dialect:

If one believes Herodotus
Arabia was once green with palms
The only place in the universe
Where cassia flourished, incense and myrrh
Laudanum and cinnamon.

Theophrastus wrote that incense and myrrh
Grew side by side and Pliny proposed
Another impossibility. He said
These disparate things
Were wept by the same tree.

The men who harvested the sacred groves
Were forbidden to touch their wives . . .
But only for the season of the harvest.
Incense fills the hand like a woman's breast.
Like love it is ephemeral.

Myrrh, too, weeps milk.
Like the stars its fruit are of unequal size.
Myrrh, too, is gathered by abstentious men
Then it is taken to a temple
The most sacred in Saba.

A part of the gum is given to the sun:
A gift for that most volatile body, the sun.

As he sings, the world dissolves, and when the song is over it is midday; they are embraced by silence. At last she sighs deeply and says, "Baba. Such a wonderful song! An ancient song—or so it seems—and a learned song. How did you come by it?"

"The song is the invention of one who came through here at the outset of the war. One who told us where to dig our new wells. Three wells so deep they touch the navel of the world. And water so fresh, so pure—although it is—he said it—an ancient water. Salt everywhere"— Belaid gestures with his arms—"but not where he told us to dig."

She follows his gaze out across the fractured, riddled land of the M'zab, little hills of salt glittering on the surface for miles. Belaid points east—

"Further there is a purple salt." She tells him that she would very much like to have some of this salt. "I will take you there," Belaid tells her, "and also to Recheg, where there is chalcedony scattered over the ground. And to Djelfa, where there are many shells turned to stone. And to the place where the golden eagle makes his nest. And to the place where I once found a needle made from the bone of a bird."

"Thank you. I would very much like to visit these places with you, Baba." She goes to the kitchen for milk and dates, two bowls, two spoons. "The song," she says when she returns. "Where did the well-digger learn it?

Did it come from the Gulf, perhaps? Was it originally Greek?"

"It was a song of his invention. He made up songs to 'animate the hours.' These are his words. He was a student of geography and geology, but also of history and politics and literature . . . in other words: a true scholar. A young man came all this way from Algiers. He is the one who told us of the insurrection."

"Here! From Algiers! How extraordinary." She rises and excitedly begins to pace. "Because, you see, I am looking for someone I knew in Zaouia in the early months of the war. He was on his way south—somewhere in the M'zab." Her breath catches: "Baba—I never knew his name. So how can I possibly find him? And then . . . I am fearful. Because I suppose he was a member of the FLN. And that this is why he could not tell me his name. Or why he was going south. Was the one who came here a member of the FLN?"

Belaid is still. He is looking into his cup as though a world were contained there.

"Baba?" She walks to him and crouches down. "Could it be the same man?" Gently she touches his sleeve. "Can you tell me his name?"

The old man continues to stare into his cup. She sees a bright tear fall from his face, making the sound of one drop of rain.

"His name was Messali," he whispers.

"Messali!" Her heart is leaping. "Messali."

"Achmed. His name was Achmed."

"Baba," she says. "I do not understand."

"His name was Abdallah." Belaid continues, his voice rising. "His name was Sayyid. His name was Mafoul. His name was Abdelaziz. He was held for a month in El-Biar. He was tortured every day for a month in El-Biar. . . ."

Trembling, she gently tugs at his sleeve. His eyes are welling over, the tears flooding his face.

"Her name was Lâlia," he says softly. "Her name was Jatchi. Her name was Shwa'wish. . . ." And Belaid screams, a terrible scream that rending the air causes all the dogs of Berriane to awaken from their midday slumber and to howl. She leans over and holds him in her arms tenderly as she would a father, a brother, a lover, a son. Rocking back and forth and speaking softly as if in prayer, Belaid whispers:

"These are the names, honored friend, I did not say aloud. I held them in my heart and was silent, even though they put the wire deep into my body. And these are the ones who died in pain despite my silence. If I survived it is only because they thought me too old to kill."

✍

That night she bathes her body slowly. She fills a large bowl with water. She rubs every inch of her body with a rough cloth. She bathes every inch of her body with water. She wonders if there will ever be enough water.

The Foxed Mirror

for Tracy Brown

Not much older than three, Guillermo is being held above a glass coffin. Beneath him lies the Christ, ribs and knee bones exposed. Guillermo's mother urges him to kiss the glass and when he refuses, twisting and arching his back, she grabs his head by the hair and forces his face down until his nose and mouth are pressed so close he cannot breathe.

All the way home he screams, refusing to be comforted, spitting bile. Ever after the world will seem flat and colorless, its asperities rubbed away as with sandpaper. Guillermo will walk a straight road beneath an indifferent sky. Desireless and willing to fulfill his mother's dreams, and despite a vague but persistent disgust he can never fathom nor explain, he will study for the priesthood, and at the age of nineteen walk to the village of Niñopan—first to assist and then to replace the swiftly deteriorating Father Cleofas, who wears a rusty cassock stained with his morning egg.

Although the air of early summer is warm and golden, when Guillermo arrives in Niñopan he is chilled to the bone. Father Cleofas appears beaming and unkempt, and with the cordial but absentminded brevity that will characterize their association, gives Guillermo a tour of the premises. Guillermo sees that the churchyard needs water; its many clay pots hold dying laurel trees. But the little church is filled with fresh flowers, and the familiar smells of roses and hot tallow put him at ease.

Under the supervision of mendicant friars, the church had been built in the early sixteenth century by Indian workmen who had managed to subvert the Christian iconography with charming and mysterious examples of indigenous and sacred forms of animals and plants. The wood ceiling over the nave is carved with skulls and butterflies. Recently the church has captured the attention of historians, and a national competition has been announced: painters under thirty years of age have been urged to contend for the honor of supplying the church—its paintings long ago destroyed by saltpeter and worms—with the fourteen stations of the cross. Sent to Mexico City for evaluation, examples of the contenders' work will be judged by a bishop, a famous painter, and the wife of a general. Pointing again and again to the bare walls, freshly whitewashed,

Father Cleofas speaks of little else. But finally the tour is over and Guillermo is taken to his quarters, a little one-room structure of stone at the far end of the churchyard. The room contains an iron bed, a wretched table, a chair, and a low cupboard in which he finds an oil lamp, a pitcher of fresh water standing in a basin, and a piece of mirror to shave by. He has brought his own soap from home wrapped in a square of clean linen.

Picking up the mirror, Guillermo gazes sadly into his face. He has inherited his mother's looks. Even as a young woman she had been too plump, her powdered face puffy like unbaked bread, her eyes overly big, the eyes of a bereaved cow, angry and perplexed. That fat white face, those looming eyes, beetling brow, and uncompromising mouth have thus far assured them both unsparing solitude. His father had been handsome and frivolous, a lover of laughter. Strangely, or perhaps not so strangely, he had vanished after only a few years of married life. His name was Severo Vertiz Salas—the only thing Guillermo knows about him. Growing up he had thought the name wonderful—*Severo Vertiz Salas*—and had repeated it over and over in his mind like an incantation in order to conjure sleep, recognizing even as a child that in his mother's house this incantation, so like a serpent's hiss, was extreme subversion.

When Guillermo was six years old he found a small silver cigar case that had—or so he imagined—belonged to his father. That night he took it to bed and as he whispered his father's name caressed the case between his fingers. Over time the case—which had been highly decorated—became smooth, its water lilies and sirens almost invisible. One night when he reached for the case it was gone. Taking up his own sex like a damp lily and causing it to rise and fill his hand with fire, he caressed it instead. But because he could not utter his father's name and caress himself at the same time, he ceased to invoke it. Shortly thereafter he left home to study for the priesthood. It did not discourage him when those in charge of his instruction explained the meaning of celibacy, for he thought he could manage very well in the world without embraces.

Putting away the piece of broken mirror, Guillermo thinks he is fortunate not to want love because with a face such as his, love cannot want him. Besides, the thought of a woman's thighs is terrible. He cannot imagine entering into the very place from which he was expelled at birth. It seems obscene. He thinks man's contract with nature is scandalously incestuous, forcing men to have—metaphorically at least—sexual relations with their own mothers. Why would anyone wish to return to the womb he had left behind?

In October Guillermo performs his first wedding. He and Father Cleofas are invited to dinner after. The dinner—a feast for one hundred people—takes place in the Crepúsculo, an inn fitted out like a chapel with windows and doors of stained glass. The motifs are secular: idealized fruits and flowers filling stylized vases or cornucopias in mutable sequences. The Crepúsculo has a glass ceiling also, illumed by lanterns of metal and glass, and whenever windows and doors are absent, mirrors hang so that the great oval room seems built upon transparencies, wholly ethereal, even when grounded by the smells of overheated bodies, *posole,* and *albóndigas reales.* Stuck to the sleeve of the old priest like a clod of earth, Guillermo feels foolish and dazed; waiters appear to revolve about the room in one direction and musicians in another as they pierce the air with birdcalls and the cries of amorous coyotes. Beside him, Cleofas, already too drunk to use a knife and fork, prods his *mole* with his fingers. Elbows on the table, Guillermo closes his eyes behind his hands and wonders if God has made him insane. Life he knows is a torment: that is the nature of space and time. But if the torment is insupportable, wouldn't one be better off dead? And if such a thought is sacrilege, why has God placed it in his head?

This is a beautiful room, he reminds himself, *and I am hearing music and conversation. I have just finished a generous helping of the best green* mole *I have ever eaten. I am sitting next to the priest I am about to replace and I have just been served a fresh piece of cake iced with white frosting and I love white frosting. So why, Lord, do I feel like taking poison?* Guillermo cuts into his cake, licks the prongs of his fork, is stunned by the sudden sweetness, and then, leaning back, looks across the room into a mirror that rises from floor to ceiling, its entire surface badly foxed. Reflected in that mirror as though through a curtain of gold lace, Guillermo sees the marvelous face and form of a youth about his own age who is entertaining a group of children by spinning a top on his own open palm. As he gazes at the top, which is wheeling like a green planet, his eyes shine with a concentrated fire that in an instant dispels Guillermo's dark mood. *The boy is like a living flame,* Guillermo thinks. *If I could meet him that would change everything!*

Deep within the mirror, the children are jumping up and down in their chairs with excitement, for now the youth has rolled up his sleeve and set more tops spinning along the length of his arm. Tossing back a mane of black hair, his eyes flashing, he looks like a matador, like Adonis. *O! The little alchemist!* Guillermo breathes, transformed.

"Saturnino!" a child cries out, his voice rising above the general din. "Let me roll back your other sleeve and set the rest to spinning!" But before this comes to pass, the old priest has wet himself and needs to be helped from the room, swiftly and discreetly. As Guillermo leads Cleofas around the musicians and into the street he bites his tongue with rage.

"You old fool!" he scolds. "What must God think of you?"

"God no longer thinks of me," Cleofas sputters, leaning on Guillermo to keep himself from falling; "now he only has thoughts for you."

That night, embraced by a scarlet mystery, Guillermo

imagines the youth, Saturnino, caressing him. Captivated he imagines the world has not abandoned him, after all, and the next day discovers more: the boy's name is Saturnino Atl and he is a leading contender for the painting prize.

ശ

Guillermo has never looked at paintings seriously, not even the one which—in his church of few treasures—provides inspiration. The painting is dark, overvarnished, and insipid, and its stiff figures could be studies after wax or plaster. Suspended at the center, a blue virgin seems heretically spineless. Weeks elapse, Guillermo roaming the streets hoping to catch sight of Saturnino Atl until his excitement gives way to a profound conviction of error. The lively impulse the painter had awakened dies. Guillermo fulfills his duties without interest, thinking to live out his life in obscurity and morbid dullness. He leads his flock—*campesinos* for the most part—telling them that their president, Porfirio Díaz, is a servant of peace and order—which is another way of saying a servant of God. He hears confession, administers absolution, and catalogs the contents of the church's cupboards and closets, counting and sorting candles of tallow and beeswax, the large and small, and all toothed by mice. But then comes the news longed for and feared: Saturnino Atl has been chosen to provide the church its fourteen stations. A small, excited child on a burro invites Guillermo and Father Cleofas—now in retirement—to visit the studio on Friday the following week.

To settle his mind, and despite the burning heat of full summer, Guillermo—who has counted every candle and vase and who can extend his itemized lists no further— throws himself into garden work, pulling up dead plants and cutting away withered foliage, renewing the exhausted earth of the potted laurels with alluvial soil taken from the lakeside in a wheelbarrow. By week's end the garden's vigor, for the most part illusory because grown in vessels of clay set upon a sandy ground, is restored. Friday comes. Taking up his broken mirror, Guillermo shaves himself with care, taking satisfaction in features browned and, he imagines, rendered serene and strengthened by the week's activity. He is anything but serene, however. He wants Saturnino to himself but Cleofas remains a permanent fixture in the church of Niñopan, and on the way to the studio Guillermo trails the old priest angrily. Cleofas is stunned with wine, and his old toes, thickened and yellow with horn, sprout like endives from his sandals. Guillermo has no choice but to plunge on after him thinking murderous thoughts.

As they enter doors wide open to the sunlit courtyard, the painter is moving in a landscape stunning in strangeness. A painter's wand in his hand, Saturnino turns away from his easel and comes toward them, blazing a trail through a wilderness of jars bristling with brushes and knives and indescribable matter: burnt orange, lemon yellow, a luminous green, an unearthly white. *How strange the air . . .* Guillermo thinks when with a wild beating of wings the pigments, varnishes, and oils fly like bees up his nose. He begins to sneeze so violently he has no choice but, his face in his sleeve, to run out again. For a time he sits on the doorstep blinking at the rim of a stone pool from which he can hear the intermittent croakings of frogs. He might have wept with shame had Saturnino not appeared, a canvas under each arm. These he places along the courtyard wall. The sky washes over them, making them shine.

"A solar day," Saturnino says as if to himself, before moving through a shaft of light and back into the studio for more. "Father Cleofas has asked to see the stations of the cross," he says, returning almost at once, "but I've only just begun. The competition was won with something dramatic but banal, a *pietà,* wildly sentimental. These are different. And the stations . . . Well, they shall be black gems, rubies from Hell!"

Attentive to the painter's every move, Guillermo stands silently by, fingering the cloth of his cassock, the bones of his face aching. The courtyard is shot through and through with color now, swarming with abundance. Cleofas wanders about looking bewildered. "You must be a genius," he says to Saturnino Atl, "because I don't understand a thing." He shuffles off and once he is gone, Guillermo sighs with pleasure. Coming closer Saturnino looks into Guillermo's eyes with unexpected heat.

"And you?" he smiles, charming and ironical. "Do you think I'm a genius too?"

Burned raw Guillermo tears himself from those eyes and leans toward the first painting as into a pure flame. It is a triptych hinged together and painted on wood. At the center is a scene of the crucifixion on the hill, but distant; the three crosses are barely visible. The theme of the painting is Christ's blood and it takes the form of a river leading down from Golgotha, a river of blood forming a deep pool, so deep that when Guillermo's eyes reach the lower third of the painting the hill is revealed to be an island floating in a lake, eerily luminous: the blood suffuses the scene with a livid glow. This lake of bloody fire is an animating fluid so compelling Guillermo is transfixed for a long while. When at last he shifts his gaze to the triptych's left panel, he sees Saturn sitting on a throne of lucid bones. In one hand he holds the scythe with which he emasculated his father, Uranus; in the other he holds his own infant son whom he is about to devour. This painting is also informed by fire: the throne gives off an eerie light and behind it the sky bristles with comets, flashes of lightning, blazing stars.

Guillermo is held in thrall by the juxtaposition of Christian and pagan themes, a heretical conjunction and dangerous. To the right Saturnino has painted the Tower of

Babel; it appears to be erupting like a volcano. At its base fire-eaters vomit sheaves of flame: the muddled languages of men have become fire, a polluting fire, thick with smoke.

When Guillermo's eyes return to Saturn and his eerie throne, the painter explains: "The ancients believed if you rattled the bones of lions they would ignite." And indeed, as Guillermo looks he sees that the earth beneath the throne is fissured and shaking. Saturn's throne stands upon a ground in upheaval; those bones *are* rattling!

"I've been told the temptation of the marvelous—" Guillermo says breathlessly, "is the temptation of—"

"Illumination." Saturnino Atl finishes the sentence for him.

"Vertigo!" Guillermo corrects him. "Delirium!"

"Exactly!" Saturnino Atl laughs. "There is no illumination without vertigo. Without delirium!"

Guillermo approaches the next picture. It is a *martirio de San Sebastián,* and the arrows piercing the saint's flesh are so sharp and swift Guillermo can hear them strike bone. The flesh swells around the shafts like ravening lips; *the arrows,* he thinks with a shudder, *are being received with hunger.* Stirred by the painting, Guillermo gnaws his knuckles in excitement, and sees a draped figure surge from the shadows behind the martyred saint, holding a scarlet cloth as if to hide him from the eyes of the crowd. Another smaller figure further back, enigmatic and nearly concealed by shadow, offers Guillermo a glass of blood like a ruby wine. The glass, like the throne of bones, illumines the entire scene.

"—And the temptation of the marvelous is the temptation of violence," says Saturnino Atl, his voice soft and mocking. Guillermo thinks this must be so. He thinks: *The marvelous may be a place where the spirit breathes.*

One after another Guillermo gazes at Saturnino Atl's astonishing paintings, one moment feeling vivid and inspired, scandalized the next. Looking at fire Guillermo burns; looking at water he drowns. The earth Saturnino has painted is not mineral, not organic, but a treacherous stuff from some other world. And when he paints air, it is so congested with sparks and the voices of angels it is unbreathable.

Gasping, Guillermo steps back as if scorched. As he looks into the painter's face his admiration and longing are so unmistakable that Saturnino approaches him and placing the back of his hand gently to Guillermo's mouth says:

"Do you wish to fuck me, little priest?" And when Guillermo, fascinated and immobile, says nothing, Saturnino continues with sinuous intensity: "Come then, little raven. I'll fuck your heart." He insinuates his hand between Guillermo's thighs.

"I!" Guillermo cries, falling against Saturnino as a frightened child falls against its mother's breast. "I am so afraid!"

"Good!" Saturnino laughs, pushing him away and then gently taking him by the shoulders. "This way it will be even better. But I warn you," he says, gravely, leading Guillermo into the gathering shadows of the garden, "I have an unfettered soul. I belong to no one." Drunk with delight, Guillermo does not entirely believe him. "The temptation of the marvelous," Saturnino laughs gently, "is inconstancy." And caressing Guillermo's naked breast and arms: "How plump you are! Like a girl! A fat little hen!" He bites Guillermo just above a nipple, making a small bruise that persists before vanishing.

When Guillermo leaves the garden he enters into a void and knows that void will be his until he is once more with Saturnino Atl. He is tempted to turn back but knows that to do so would be a grave error. He must not weigh upon Saturnino; what has happened in a state of grace may not be possible to duplicate. But he has entered into the painter's gravitational system as it were, and if he returns to the void, it is a void tilted toward Saturnino so that he needs to do battle with himself to keep from retracing his steps and turning up the cobbled road that leads to the studio. He suppresses the impulse although it causes him pain, fearing that any action he might take will lead to catastrophe. He lives the next few days in segments as though he could in this way reshape time and make its passing bearable. But even then the pattern of the minutes and hours is tediously slow, like the formation of tree rings, the wearing away of mountains.

If I don't return, Guillermo thinks, *I will become as precious to him as he is to me. If I don't return.* And this thought becomes an incantation with which he charms himself, a prayer: *If I don't return.* And then: *I will not return.* Time drags along, until Guillermo has celebrated a year of holy days.

One summer morning a child on a burro, perhaps the same child Saturnino had sent before but taller now, informs Guillermo that the stations of the cross have been completed and that Saturnino Atl wishes to deliver them the next day. Guillermo receives this news as a violent intrusion; time gathers speed as does his blood and all that night he thrashes about in the hot ocean evoked by the painter's memory: violent, yes, and vertiginous, yes; illuminating, also.

A clatter of hooves and iron wheels announces the painter's arrival. Guillermo stands before his church, the doors open wide, the altar bright with roses. In one spellbinding gesture, Saturnino leaps from the carriage followed by a wild company of young men, each one as lithe, as witching as he, their hair tumbling to their shoulders like clusters of purple grapes, their dark eyes sparking the air. They all wear white shirts open at the throat, riding boots. *Like*

actors! Guillermo thinks with growing terror; *like gypsies!* Taking down paintings and surging toward him, Guillermo wonders what and who they are, so unlike the tame flock he is used to tending. *Like wild geese!* Apprentices? Models? Or Saturnino Atl's lovers? Something tells him these are lovers. Because of their beauty. Because their eyes mock him. Because they fill the courtyard with catcalls and howling. When the painter passes the priest he clucks like a hen, evoking raucous laughter.

Guillermo flees up the rood stairs to the rood tower and there, although he is not aware of it, gnaws his knuckles and wrings his hands. He thinks: *I am a coward. Saturnino Atl was right to have insulted me just now.* Hadn't the painter given him the only hour of pleasure he had ever known? And how had Guillermo responded? By hiding out! By killing time!

Later, when the commotion and the laughter have ceased, when the hammering and shouts come no more, nor the sound of the ladder being pulled across the stone floor; when the horses' hooves and the carriage wheels are only a memory, and long after the dust has settled in the road; later, when the moon and the stars have risen and Guillermo descends into the church and lights all the candles, the cheap and the dear, and gazes intently at the fourteen incidents of Christ's passion in succession, he knows his own humiliation is scarcely like this.

The Neurosis of Containment

for Dorothy Wallace

What I am about to relate took place in the late summer of 1930 when, a woman of middle age, I was a guest at the house of Mrs. Livesday in Barrytown-on-Hudson. The house was destroyed the following year in a freak storm that lasted under an hour and yet devastated the village and woodland. No one was harmed, and Mrs. Livesday, her vigor untrammeled, simply took up house-keeping in her summer home on Block Island—not a small feat for a woman in her eighties.

A self-taught student of botany, I had spent the previous summer in Mrs. Livesday's company on the island, hunting down rare specimens and pressing them between prepared papers. I also collected seeds—upon Mrs. Livesday's encouragement: of field poppy, chickweed, nigella, et cetera;

and pinecones, the samara of the maple and elm. Some seeds are smooth and others rough and wrinkled; the seed of the field poppy is honeycombed with alveolate depressions. I set the seeds in cotton from the pharmacy.

Although a Christian and a woman of common sense, Mrs. Livesday had been reading the Jew, Freud. Certain arcane words and phrases—cabalistic, very pagan—peppered her conversation—always lively—so that speaking with her was now more than ever like eating borscht. That summer on Block Island I heard for the first time *psychical unpleasure* and *obsessional neurotic.* And although these terms were addressed to me—"There goes Gertrude Hubble once again indulging in psychical unpleasure!" or, "May I introduce you to my friend Gertrude Hubble, one of my favorite obsessional neurotics?"—they were always said with an affectionate tone. In other words, I did not take Mrs. Livesday's latest enthusiasm seriously. (I believe it is a mistake to take Jewish ideas seriously.) When I came down to dinner with my boxes of seeds neatly sown in sterile cotton in impeccable rows, Mrs. Livesday turned to Cobb—who at that moment had brought a large tureen of veal-bone broth to the table—and said: "Cobb, look at these latest efforts of Gertrude's and tell me: might they be said to illustrate a *neurosis of containment?*"

Despite the fact that I, too, am Christian, that Mrs. Livesday was both a great deal older than myself and my hostess, my dander was up.

"These little collections," I said, "lovingly arranged are nay more than *seeds,* Mrs. Livesday. I fear your gracious mind has been addled by Semitic tomfoolery!"

"No! No!" she replied with such earnest good nature that I was at once reduced to shame. "They are charming, dear—there is no doubt about that. Very prettily executed. You do everything with skill, Gertrude, and these collections are no exception to *that* rule. But, you see, Cobb and I were talking in the kitchen about *pathological phenomena*" (inwardly I rolled my eyes, my temper fraying anew) "and how anxiety is often revealed by attempts to order and to contain the world. Anxiety is the product of chaos—or, rather, of the *fear* of chaos—and what could be more chaotic than the natural world? So we attempt to order it: just look at Cobb's spice rack! Yes! Yes! I *know* I'm being silly. But, for example, think of the way you lay out your combs and brushes as though they were schoolchildren or dead matter: bones, fossil fish on exhibit in a museum! One, two, three—run up to your dresser, Gertrude, and there they will be! Lined up: big brush, little brush, comb next—lined up as if for execution! Don't look at me like that. So are your shoes!"

I was scandalized. How did she know about my shoes? I was outraged. Cobb offered to serve me a slice of chicken pie and despite its fragrancy I shook my head, frowning for all I was worth.

"You are wanting *pleasure,* Gertrude." Mrs. Livesday

prodded her butler on. "Do serve our guest some pie. It is too easy to ruffle your feathers, my dear," she said kindly. "And so that you won't think otherwise, I didn't go up to your room to spy. Call it intuition!"

"I was brought up to be an orderly person," I said next. "Nothing to be ashamed of."

"Yes! Yes!" She tore into her bread with such ferocity I was startled. "But suppose it all *means something*." I was dumbfounded, my temples throbbing. "Suppose those shoes and those brushes in their rigorous rows, and the perfectly folded linens in the upper-left-hand drawer were the key to your inviolable soul, Gertrude. Saying more about you than anything you could possibly say about yourself?"

The rest of that week I roamed the crags of Block Island collecting pebbles and wondering about Mrs. Livesday. Had she gone mad? What had hairbrushes to do with spirit? Clearly hairbrushes, linens, and shoes were worldly artifacts. Once I attempted to squelch her for good by saying in my most imperious tone: "There are no linens, hairbrushes, or combs in Heaven!"

"Poor creature," had been her response, before retracting into a silence unlike her. "No. I suppose not." Before we separated for the night she addled me one last time: "Gertrude," she said, "why were you never a flapper? Had I been your age . . ." She trailed off and then: "Oh! Imagine! To have been a *flapper!*"

The key to my room in Barrytown was very small—like the key to a child's music box—and when I opened the door and saw Mrs. Livesday's collection of family dolls nested down in ancient perambulators, I thought the key's size most appropriate. One of the dolls was black—a rarity in any collection. Black people were a rarity in those days, too, at least within the circle in which I moved. Missionary friends in Africa saw them in droves, of course, and once Mrs. Livesday had thrown an eccentric garden party for the Episcopal clergy and friends of the mission work to which—to my astonishment and discomfiture—a number of Negroes came. As I had previously offered to pour, I found myself in the preposterous position of pouring tea for potential cannibals.

Mrs. Livesday's black poppet was a pretty thing, idealized, its expression sweet and its clothes—if faded with age—trim. As with her tea guests, not one button was missing from the little shirt and trousers; the doll even wore shoes. I am a spinster, and it occurred to me that putting me up in this particular room demonstrated a certain insensitivity on Mrs. Livesday's part.

In a recent letter, my dear friend Deacon Hill, who was living among the Kaffirs in Kaffirland, described the marriage customs of that country and included a little sketch of Oz, the chief of the Zulus, in ordinary dress—or, dare I say it, *undress*—for as far as I could tell, Mr. Oz wore little else than a feather duster. I recall being not a little surprised when I opened Deacon Hill's envelope and the sketch fell out. The sketch proved Deacon Hill's imperfect judgment—the result, I suppose, of living among savages for longer than any civilized person should. I was outraged. But his letter proved fascinating and I read it despite myself. The Deacon described domestic polity in Kaffirland and I learned that Oz, who perambulated in nothing but a handful of turkey feathers, had an illimitable number of wives! The Deacon had enclosed a photograph: a gaggle of wives all sitting on their heels in rows, bowls of porridge incongruously set before them—perhaps to illustrate a racial propensity for overindulgence. Standing among several dozen dolls, all white and female but for one little black fellow trussed up in striped trousers, I could not help but think I had been spirited away to a Kaffir harem—a conceit I imagined would surely amuse Deacon Hill as I was a spinster of forty-two with no intention of marrying, not ever. In his letter the Deacon instructed me that in Kaffirland each wife has her own hut.

"Tell Oz," I wrote to Deacon Hill that evening in reply, "that I am already an integral member of a harem in Barrytown and have no intention of giving my heart to Oz—even though he has apparently (reading between the lines) offered me a hut of my very own and, as I gather from the photograph, my very own bowl of porridge, and even though it is all too true that my own Bambola has *his* harem packed together in one small room—two or three to a perambulator!"

That night I was plagued by a peculiar ringing deep within my left ear—or, perhaps, the brain. It was impossible to tell although I concentrated on it for hours. The absurd question how many angels can dance on a pin came to mind although it was easier to imagine infinitesimal devils wearing tin shoes and crashing cymbals any which way. Once I had that idea—of devils cavorting within my inner ear, or tucked away in a corner of my brain—I was submerged by anxiety and unable to sleep. Turning on the bedside light, I was further dismayed by the sight of Mrs. Livesday's dolls, their porcelain eyes smoldering in the shadows.

When at last I slept—and this thanks to a summer shower, soothed as I was by the patter of rain upon the roof and the windowpanes—I dreamed unpleasant dreams apparently, for I awoke troubled, my temper frayed, the strange words *Time's flies* buzzing in my mind. I recalled that the old cemetery was just beyond Mrs. Livesday's garden and what else could Time's flies be but the things that swarm about a cadaver? I feared I breathed a tainted atmosphere and got out of bed to take from my travel case a bottle of fine cologne. I dabbed at my temples, deeply inhaling, before, exhausted, falling back upon my pillow, thinking to catch a few minutes' repose before breakfast. And then I heard it again and it came to me that I might be the aural witness to the wheels of my own thought—the *genesis* of thought, so to speak. But were this the case, those wheels needed greasing, for the brittle clashing was chaotic—no rhythm discernible at all. Yet it was persistent—busy and incalculable as bacilli. This noise was a poisonous thing, demanding all my attention. I sent my mind ranging through the week's occupations: tasks performed, books read, conversations with my sister, et cetera, and yet always came back to that infernal chamber music. And whether my pulse stilled or quickened, the clatter had a life of its own and paid my pulse no mind.

The sun had long been up and I had arranged to meet my hostess at seven-thirty for breakfast. I chose a white linen blouse and a beige linen skirt—both in need of pressing—scrubbed my face until it shone pink, pulled a comb through my hair, and put on a pair of comfortable shoes as it was a habit of Mrs. Livesday's to take a long walk after breakfast.

Breakfast was always sumptuous—Cobb bringing out a great silver platter of eggs scrambled with oysters, piping hot coffee, and fresh bread. When Mrs. Livesday noticed that my appetite was not equal to her own, I described for her as best I could the wee cacophony plaguing me. I was mortified when, as Cobb returned with a freshly made compote of summer apples, she asked him to fetch the ear syringe, for she supposed my discomfort was the result of accumulated wax. I thanked her curtly, informing her that I was not accustomed to having men aware of or engaged in my intimate affairs. Just then Cobb returned with the thing—bright red it was and seemed far too large for the office with which it was to be entrusted.

"Warm salt water," said Cobb. "I've placed a basin in the upstairs lavatory." I blushed. Once he was gone, Mrs. Livesday, with an odd bark, said, "Well! I never thought I'd see the day when Cobb—poor old Cobb!—would make a woman blush! And over an *ear*—! It's not as though he'd handed you an amorous proposal!" I was shocked. Never in all our time together had I ever heard Mrs. Livesday suggest a vulgarity. In more soothing tones she continued: "Do give it a good flushing, and then we will take our walk and I will tell you about Freud and you will tell me about your sister and Deacon Hill's latest letter, and all the things that have transpired since we were last together!"

Enraged with her, I kept an outward appearance of calm and did as she asked. The cymbals were clashing and the little hooves clattering, and when I reached the lavatory I dropped the basin to the tiles, where it shattered, bringing Cobb at once with another basin, a large mop, a dustpan, and a broom. As he bent over the small mess I had caused, I thought that, indeed, he was not much of a man. One could not imagine him in any function other than the one he had—that of butler, cook, and companion to an old, an eccentric woman.

"Cobb!" I said. "Do you do the ironing, too?" And as

his answer was satisfactory, I gave him what I had brought but for the clothes I wore—everything horribly creased despite the care I had taken, packing it all between sheets of tissue paper.

∽

It was later, on our walk together, that I heard a trill of peculiar intensity, a series of notes sweetly piercing. Next I saw close by the path a remarkably beautiful bird, slender-beaked, its wings a velvety black with emerald markings as though embroidered there, its breast a glittering steel blue, its tail velvet. Indeed it seemed to me so lovely that I imagined it had flown directly to Barrytown from Paradise. Again it called and then, spreading its wings, was gone with such celerity I was astonished.

I cried out to Mrs. Livesday, who at that moment was off the path examining a clump of wild asparagus with the intent to pirate it for lunch, and who came running—too late to see the marvelous bird. She had no idea what it was I had seen and supposed it was a raven: the velvety black, the metallic reflection. . . . Once again I felt myself flush with anger.

"But," I insisted, "the song was superb!"

"I don't disbelieve you," she countered. "However, the raven imitates the cries of other birds—a marvelous thing in itself." And she was off, as was her wont, this time telling of Dr. Franklin's raven Jacob who could imitate the cries of infants, the crowing of cocks. As she spoke, the ringing in my ear, until then blessedly absent, thrust me into an agitation impossible to conceal.

∽

My sister Abigail had been a flapper and when she returned home at dawn dressed in what looked like a slip our family dissolved. Mother, who had been waiting up for her, slapped her as soon as she walked through the door. This fact was the one major event that undid everything, for rather than burst into tears, or run to her room and lock herself in, or implore forgiveness, or attempt the impossible: to justify the levity (and that is putting it politely), she turned on her heel and vanished (and she was wearing a pair of silver shoes such as I had never seen). We had no news of her for years.

Once she was picked up downtown for vagrancy and if Father paid her bail he did not attempt to see her. That week he removed her from his will. A few years later when both Mother and Father were carried away by influenza, I was sole inheritress of a modest allowance that has enabled me to live comfortably—if carefully—the life of a gentlewoman of an earlier time and not have to scrounge for a living teaching other people's brats—the work for which I was trained—or to submit to the banalities and indignities of matrimony.

After Abigail vanished, Mother, Father, and I did our

best to fill the hole she had left behind—"with good, black earth," Mother said, "a heavy stone on top."

At first we entertained a hushed silence—never speaking of her, nor for that matter, of much of anything. We kept busy at our separate tasks, although I must admit I often pretended to be busy. But then little by little we began to speak together again and—as if by silent consent—to re-create the past *sans* Abigail. This involved a great deal of concentration and imagination. It became a game as well as an act of faith, or I should say: love. For in this way we were able to reassure one another and to prove that our affection was real, somehow legitimate (as if *that* needed to be proved!) and that we were worthy of being called a family. The unexpected effect of all this tender subterfuge was that I learned to speak convincingly and with elo- quence on just about anything and so to contribute to important causes—such as Deacon Hill's charities. And if Mrs. Livesday has chided me about what she calls my "an- tiquated manner" and "eccentricities of speech," I pride myself upon this capacity. I see myself not only as Christ's spokeswoman, but a servant of Good English. Before Abi- gail vanished, her conversation rattled and belched with absurdist "slang."

"What news," Mrs. Livesday asked as we returned the way we had come up the path, "have you of your sister?"

"Abigail is beyond repair," I answered her, and with such acidity that Mrs. Livesday, if she frowned, did not dare ask me about my sister again. Perhaps because of my curt reply, lunch was eaten in silence, and after coffee Mrs. Livesday retired.

Sometime in midafternoon as I lay in my chamber in an attempt to refresh my brain, I heard her depart with Cobb for town (a salmon had been ordered from the city for our supper) and overheard the following; it stabbed me to the quick:

Cobb: *Is Miss Hubble coming with us?*

Mrs. Livesday: *Good gracious, no! She'd spoil our fun. Let's steal away, Cobb. Now!*

Well what of it if I had been brusque. She was, after all, an intrusive busybody who had no right, no right whatsoever, to bring up family matters out of the blue. And now the dreadful poppets were all gazing at me, or so it seemed, with eager eyes. "Tell Oz," I continued the letter to the Deacon in my head, "that the Barrytown harem is beginning to test my temper." I closed my eyes.

The trilling was deeper now; it had gathered energy and speed. Overtaken by exhaustion, it seemed to me that a blizzard of sound was raging in my skull, so that when I slept I dreamed of ice. In my dream I was struggling along a narrow isthmus hemmed in on all sides by ice. I knew that I needed to head south, else die, and prayed for the sun to guide me. And then I saw it blazing before me beyond a veil of snow and sleet. As I battled on I could hear the ice falling with a fearful distinctness, but the sun was fuller now; it began to blaze with such intensity I feared as much for my life as before. The sun's shape was strange—more like a vertical mouth—and I knew with rage and horror that it was not the sun at all but Abigail's vulva burning above my face.

I awoke then, shuddering and drenched with perspiration. The sun was sinking; low on the horizon it had, for an instant, flooded the room. I lay panting until it had set, until I lay in shadow, until the first crickets began their chirping—so shocked by the vision in the dream that I prayed: *Let me be turned to stone this instant!* For that is precisely what I thought I deserved—to be rendered blind and deaf and mute. But instead of turning to stone, I lay hot and heavy on the bed until I heard a sound beyond those of evening, beyond, even, the ringing of my mind, a sound akin to the rustle of dry leaves in the wind or the sensuous rasp a taffeta gown makes on the body of an actress as she moves across the stage; a sound of such intense sweetness that my heart was at once throbbing with a rare delight. A delicious sound and captivating—and yet chilling because so *feral.* A wild, extravagant murmur unlike anything I had ever heard before. I raised myself from my pillow then and stared at the door expectantly. I should not have been surprised had Pan himself walked into the room. I waited. Nothing out of the ordinary occurred except that once the moment had passed I felt an acute sense of loss, or longing—I cannot say which—as though something offered had been taken back.

Because I had to, I next bathed and dressed, did my hair, and, succumbing to a rare moment of vanity, pulled out some silver by the roots. I thought: *My eyes are still quite fine.* Opening the lavatory door I heard a familiar domestic clatter, the table being set deep within the house, the oven door opening and closing, and made my way down two flights of stairs to the first floor, which was brightly lit and submerged in the fragrant smells of Cobb's excellent cooking.

I found Mrs. Livesday in the music room sipping sherry.

"And have you rested?" she asked with what I feared was forced cordiality.

"I have, thank you," I replied, "and I must apologize to you. Please accept my apology, Mrs. Livesday. You have always shown me nothing but generosity and have been a constant friend now for over a decade—"

"That long! Of course I accept. What a relief! Dear Gertrude, you *have* been testy. But now that's over and forgotten. Have some sherry and begin to think about the feast Cobb has prepared." Indeed, as I had lain thrashing in my little room, they had been to the train station to fetch a large, boxed fish packed in ice and sent from Nova Scotia. It was a beautiful salmon, its recent history revealed on a small square of cardboard Cobb had found tucked playfully in its smiling mouth. There were lemons in the box also— an extravagance in those days—wrapped in white paper. And they had also brought back flowers—something I wished I had thought of myself. *Instead of stewing upstairs,* I chided myself, *I might have been out gathering flowers.* Entering the dining room with Mrs. Livesday on my arm and

seeing them throbbing at the table's center I said as much:
"I *intended* to bring you some flowers, dearest Mrs. Livesday!" (I had not thought to bring her anything!) "But I
promise to make up for my ill temper and the rest."

"Dear Gertrude!" she replied. "Will you please cease to
torture yourself! Now. Sip this wine and look! Here
comes Cobb with our fish." Baked in cream, it appeared to
swim in a dish the size of a small pool. Cobb brought out
scalloped potatoes next, a spinach soufflé, corn bread. "Attempt to discover the nature of our dessert," she continued, "although I doubt you can!"

Cobb sat down then and smiling shyly echoed her: "I
doubt she can!"

I could not. As it turned out, Cobb had baked a tarte
Tatin—and a perfect one, I should add, gilded with caramel and served with a small glass of brandy, followed by a
smaller cup of Turkish coffee.

"Mine shows a face!" Mrs. Livesday cried, peering into
her cup. "The world is full of delights." She gave Cobb
her brandy glass to be refilled, repeating as she took it back:
"To delight!"

Again I felt stirring that irresistible rage. I believed she
was chiding me for my spinsterhood and Spartan ways and
so set to scowling, muddling over a thousand things, as the
eerie buzzing started up again—or I became once more
aware of it.

She: *It seems the word* delight *has offended you, somehow.*
I: *Not at all! Delight! How could it? That would be silly!* I

blushed. *It's only . . . my ear is still ringing . . . a strange affliction . . . hard to describe. Imagine a hive, Mrs. Livesday, filled with bees made of tin. Bees the size of . . . atoms. Their wings . . . cymbals of brass. Imagine that! Deep in your brain! I wonder: Could I have picked up some malady on the train?*

She: *Poor Gertrude! I had completely forgotten. So you are still afflicted with this odd malaise. I hope it is not tinnitus! Or Ménière's disease. My God! That would be terrible! Do you feel dizzy? Nauseous? Your appetite is good. That is a promising sign. Shall we call in a doctor? I've a competent one just down the road.*

Astonishing us both I blurted out: "But I do not wish to be cured! What if this is . . . is *intentional?*"

"Intentional?"

"A summons of some sort."

"Gertrude! A *summons!* Forgive me but I cannot follow your reasoning here. A summons from whom?"

"But I have no idea!" I cried out, my irritation rising once again. Why was she always demanding that I justify myself? "You are worse than my mother!"

"That I doubt." Had I hurt her? She looked more per-plexed than hurt.

"How *horrid* I am!" I said then. "How horrid to *you* my dearest friend and the sanest. Yes, Mrs. Livesday, the *sanest creature* I know!"

"A sane creature!" She laughed. "I like that. It makes me feel like a thing from fairyland. Something Alice might have met on the train in Wonderland. *A sane creature!* What you need," she continued, "is a second glass of brandy. This one therapeutic. You are frazzled—that's clear enough, but surely not beyond repair. This will cause you to sleep and to dream," she said as she filled my glass, "and to awaken refreshed and lively, full of good spirits. Tomorrow is the flower show—do you remember? And we will enjoy a marvelous time in Rhinebeck. I've heard that the displays this year are unlike anything they've done previously. You know: the rarest blooms. It will be a treat." As she spoke I sipped my second brandy dreamily and when it was time for bed, went upstairs feeling tipsy and happier than I had in a very long time. In fact, when I reached my little room I felt so buoyant that had there been a party going on in the music room, I would have returned there and joined in the dancing, a thing I had not done for ever so long—or rather, a thing I, to be honest, had *never* done. The one who had danced was Abigail. "One too many," said Father.

For a time I stood upon the threshold staring out across the little bed, the dolls in their perambulators, and as the window was wide open to the night, out across Mrs. Livesday's south lawn flooded as it was with moonlight. The sight was so inviting, the room so small, so stifling, that I stole back down the stairs and, unlocking the music room's French doors, out into the night. For a time I stood in the center of the lawn beneath the moon, painfully aware of my unbecoming behavior. The buzzing in my ear had ceased and the only sound the gentle rustle of leaves agitated by the merest whisper of a breeze. Until I heard again, briefly, that sweet trilling, and again—preceded by a hush—that strange, troublous sound.

It was then that I saw what had been haunting me. They moved toward me precisely, inexorably, and gently also, *like naked truth* I thought; yes, there was something flawless about the way they moved across Mrs. Livesday's moon-soaked lawn: two tall, beautiful young men, redheaded and pale, moving with a species of subtlety, a rigor, a—I have difficulty finding the words—a *meticulousness* so that I was held in thrall. And they had wings—enormous, velvety wings of tawny brown and deepest black with spots of blue and green so dark and rich-looking in the moonlight. So stately were they as they moved toward me, their great wings rustling and sighing, that they might have been bishops.

And then they were so close that looking up into their faces I could see how pale their skins were, how delicate, even a little raw around their nostrils, their eyes, and at the corners of their lips, as though they had been weeping or, perhaps, just recently recovered from a malady, or had been out in the cold.

"You have summoned us," the first one said.

"I, never!"

"You dreamed the cipher," said the second. "The cipher that, in our world, is an *open sesame*." And he laughed.

"What cipher?" I whispered. They were both so beautiful I could not tear my eyes from their faces, their throbbing necks, their shoulders—which were powerful, supporting as they did the greater weight of those terrible wings.

"The cipher of sexual longing." With his fingers he traced the contours of my aging face lovingly, a tenderness that flooded me with sweetness. Yet I thought his touch sinister, too. I stepped back, and forcing myself to speak— for I was mesmerized by his touch and the heat in his eyes—

"There is no such thing as men with wings. What are you doing in Mrs. Livesday's garden? I suppose you are burglars," I said then, simultaneously fascinated and aghast, "and furthermore," I continued, fighting to get my ire up—for I was so drowsy, so submerged in something I can only—to speak clearly—describe as *longing*—"who gave you leave to touch me?"

"You gave me, gave us leave," he said. "Can you deny it?" He stepped behind me so that I was standing between the two of them, the moonlight pouring down upon us like an inverted fountain.

The closeness of those two male bodies was an astonishing thing. I felt as though I were encompassed by a halo that caused an intense lethargy to invade my soul. I attempted to disengage myself from what seemed to be an illicit embrace although they did not touch me. But when I attempted to flee from the charmed circle, the two—with the clatter of a sailboat in a high wind—spread their wings and I was held in the deviant space they made. Then, as I stood there in the curious orbit of their wings, they began to touch me with their fingers, to insinuate their warm fingers into my hair. It fell to my shoulders like water once they had loosened it from its nets and pins. Next they began to worry the buttons of my blouse. Whatever way I turned I could not escape their many hands—captive as I was between those wings. I felt a compelling ease of spirit, a vibrancy, a fluidity I had never known, and imagined this was a species of dancing. I would have succumbed to them; I was about to swoon with pleasure, their many hands on my neck, my breasts, when I realized the danger, the terrible danger I was in, the impossible danger of what I was about to do. Indeed, the one was whispering in my ear scandalously, outrageously: "I shall penetrate your cunt and my brother your ass, simultaneously as you have wished." It was the unforgivable heresy of these words that brought me to my senses and I cried out with rage: "Begone! Begone! Never to return! For I hate you! I hate you both with all my heart! I loathe your caresses! How dare you touch me!" And I screamed as loud as I was able: "Burglars! Burglars in the night!" Cobb came running—it was absurd—with a broom, and Mrs. Livesday—dressed in white, in a dressing gown that looked like white silk, the dressing gown of a bride—came running too. The fearless soul! Brandishing a poker! How I loved her at that instant, running so unafraid. Already I was in Cobb's frail arms, sobbing.

"There were two," I cried, "two burglars! Two burglars with black wings!"

"Black wings!" Mrs. Livesday began to laugh. "Black wings! Gertrude! Think what you are saying." I ceased to sob and, pulling away from Cobb, stared at Mrs. Livesday with astonishment.

"That is impossible," I said.

"Are you certain they were burglars?" Taking me by the arm she steered me back to the house as Cobb led the way with his broom. "Your hair is lovely," she said, "the color of wheat. I've never seen it down."

"I don't want to sleep in that wretched room," I blurted out, "with all those damned toys, Mrs. Livesday, as though I were, as though I were a mere, a mere child!"

"Well, you won't." She soothed me, her own brow deeply furrowed. "What a peculiar thing. Had I known . . . it's not as though I'm lacking in rooms. It's the view," she babbled now—I had succeeded in ruffling the calmest of women—"it's because it's the room with the best view. Especially now when the moon is full. That night garden! Bathed in tender light!"

I was sobbing again, uncontrollably.

"Were you harmed?" She was once more alarmed.

"Yes! I believe. I believe they wanted to"—we were in the music room now—"to invade my privacy." I had bewildered her, utterly.

"But they . . . how many were there?"

"Two."

"Did not manage to . . . 'invade your privacy'?" ("Whatever that means!" she added as an aside to Cobb.)

"No." I ceased to cry. I was ashamed of myself but I could not have said why. Because I shouted out. And Cobb came, bless him! With a broom! I laughed out loud. "And you—*dear* Mrs. Livesday—I have caused you so much trouble. You must think me mad."

"Not at all."

"And now asking for another room in the middle of the night when the little room is so delightful. What could have gotten into me?"

"I can easily put you in another room. Cobb, could you make up Puffy's old room? We call it that," she explained, "because that's where old Mrs. Notus used to stay. The children called her Puffy because of her asthma or whatever it was that plagued her. Poor thing. Emphysema. Plagued her constantly. Now she's so old. Older than I! Fit to be stuffed! Put on display!"

We had reached the room. It was stuffy, had not been aired since Puffy's last visit. I stood blinking stupidly as a moth discovered the bedside lamp and stormed the shade. Cobb bustled in with my few belongings in a jumble and wondered: Would I be needing tea? He would bring up a vase of fresh flowers in the morning. Would I be wanting breakfast in bed? Mrs. Livesday told him to stop treating me like an invalid. At last they were gone.

The room had an outsized mirror—a thing I was not accustomed to. As I disrobed I caught sight of my naked body. In the lamplight it seemed surprisingly lovely to me: full, rosy, and youthful still. Unlike my face—how it had aged! As though it had been shut away, forgotten at the back of a closet. And my eyes. My eyes were not kind at all. And they were haunted.

Fortuné

*M*y passion for Egypt was sparked at the opera. Until the night of *The Magic Flute* my dreams were so savorless they seemed to belong to another. But the palms, the Sphinx smiling like the Mona Lisa beneath the moon, had me bouncing up and down yapping: *"Wow! Wow!"*

My mistress was already famous and so I was not scolded, nor were we sent away. Instead we had inspired a brief but flattering fashion among the Incroyables: now every woman of taste was carrying a little black dog to the opera. I was distressed by this proliferation of look-alikes, for having been the only black pup in the litter, I had until then thought of myself as exceptional.

The night of *The Magic Flute* I dreamed astonishing

dreams; they fulfilled all my expectations as to what dreaming could be. After that vivid night I knew that though I
looked like any number of little dogs, I, Heaven help me,
did not *imagine* as they imagined. And this to my pride and
consternation, for I was exceedingly lonely and in the
company of my peers bored to tears when—as happened
every afternoon—I was forced to share the better part of
the day with ladies of quality and their witless pets—each
one a basket case, and this is not only because they were
carried from place to place in baskets but because of the
milk soup passing for conversation among them. And there
were terrible times when during a brief encounter in the
streets of Paris I risked being eaten alive by dogs so vicious
and gigantic it was my conviction they belonged to another species. How often I wished for a spiked collar or,
better still, an ivory tower!

But back to my dreams of the night of the opera: in
these dreams Isis predominated, Isis who like a dog has
multiple tits, Isis her name a whisper, the sound of a serpent's hiss, of hot metal plunged into cold water, of—or so
I imagine—palm trees agitated by the simoon. Even then,
before the Campaign, Isis haunted Paris, her cult showing
up in the most unexpected places, a little spooky, maybe,
but also dream-inducing, mysterious, and erotic!

So Egypt became something of an obsession with me
and caused me to fantasize during those lost hours in the
morning when my mistress prepared herself for the day,
trying on her "creoleries" for best effect and posing lasciv-

iously before her mirror—for at this time she was seducing
Boney, who, from what I gathered, was truffling after
wealth, good connections, exoticism, and glory, too. Of
course, Josephine never fooled me. I was there when she
patched her torn bloomers with thread she'd taken from
Madame Menfous's sewing box, and when she re-soled her
slippers with velvet she'd snipped from her seat at the
Opéra-Comique.

The week Boney first appeared sniffing at her skirts, an
extravagant purse given her by a lover paid for a cabinet of
island wood carved with blackamoors and bananas; in it
she displayed all she had left of silver plate—so highly polished I could see my own face in the pottingers and plat-
ters. She set this cabinet in the foyer and its effect was
spectacular. Then she invited Boney for a midnight supper
and spent the entire evening setting the scene. She heaped
the dining-room table with bottles of Madeira and bowls
of tropical fruit; she threw scarves on all the chairs, she
borrowed exotic trees from the botanical gardens, sliced
pineapples, gutted papayas, blackened her eyebrows,
rouged her cheeks, arranged her breasts in her corset like
apples in a basket, and when the clock struck twelve,
scented of jasmine, a kerchief in her hair, she uncoiled like
a mulatta on the divan. Poor Boney! He thought he had
stumbled into Paradise when in fact he had collided with a
weather vane.

When after supper Boney tipped out of his boots and
into bed with her, *I bit him*—not out of jealousy as History

has proposed, but because I wanted to warn him. *Bitten in bed!* The man was wildly superstitious and this should have been enough to indicate the trap he had fallen into. But so madly in love was he, he gently put me on the floor and proceeded to plunder Josephine with all he was worth—which, poor soul, was not much. Her mind was on someone else. (To entertain Boney like that, it would have to be.)

∽

If dogs received salaries for comforting and entertaining their mistresses and masters, why I would not squander mine on biscuits, but would build myself a little dog-sized wonder room filled with the marvels of Egypt, and why? Because in Egypt objects are not mere things but sacred signs—else why would the hieroglyphs be so packed with worldly stuff? Roast ducklings, casseroles, pipkins, bottles of beer?

∽

I have come to know Boney better. He is a man motivated by an authentic visionary mechanism of mind (and here I might add: *so like my own!*). This visionary mechanism is what has precipitated him into the good graces of Glory and more: inspired the voyage about to be undertaken, the conquest and subsequent investigation of *Wow! Wow!* all the secret marvels slumbering beneath the sands of Egypt! In other words, like me he is a dreamer, and his project, his fabulous—I should say his *Roman*—project, to seize Egypt from the Mamelukes, to pull her out from the Middle Ages and to thrust her into the Age of Reason, inspires me. The man may be precipitate and short-winded in bed, but in other things he is a giant.

I am attempting to convince my mistress to follow him to Egypt—it is the chance of a lifetime! The Industrial Revolution is just around the corner; any day now pyramids and temples will be reduced to lime and the hills of Thebes littered with bottle caps!

In my dreams I see myself asleep beneath the gaze of the Sphinx, or chasing rabbits in the palm forests of Rosetta. I imagine doing my business beneath pomegranate trees, and sitting on a camel in my own dog-sized saddle, a bright copper compass dangling from my neck—a compass always pointing North (N for Napoleon)—and in my saddlebags a magnificent magnifying glass. For I intend to study the Egyptian spider. I have always been partial to spiders. Why? Because they are as furry as fox terriers, because they wear their eyes like tiaras around their heads, because like balloonists they ride the wind. When I hear that Geoffroy Saint-Hilaire will be of the party and that he is heading a commission on the study of spiders and snakes I am beside myself! *Wow! Wow!* One hundred and sixty-seven artists and thinkers all on their way to Egypt together! Imagine the stimulation, the scintillating conversation. *Wow! Wow!* I dance on my mistress's lap and joyfully lick her fingers as Boney describes his ship's library, the books all packed in flannel-lined cases. *Flannel-lined cases!* Books on history—ancient and modern—zoology, surgery, architecture—and all *full of pictures!* Books on the manufacture of baba and bread pudding and dog biscuits, too! *"Wow!"* I say to Josephine, tugging at her sleeves with my teeth, *"Wow! Wow!"* They're taking along hot-air balloons and solid brass barometers! They will investigate the phenomenon of the mirage, live in the palaces of the exiled Mamelukes and in the shadow of Cheops, chew on barbecued lamb!

"O *Boney!*" I bark joyfully, leaping into the air. "O pomegranate seed! O lamp of crystal! *Ya salaam!* I salute you! And would gladly follow your star!"

But Josephine sits unmoved. She has not time for me, nor for Boney, either. Her mind is on her lover, a fop who has no interest in libraries and portable pianos, a wag who has no liking for astrolabes, who does not give a fig for maps; a flyspeck brain for whom the ancient world is as interesting as a spinster's dresser drawer. *Nothing* can fire this imagination. If one mentions elephants roaming in wild tribes in Nubia, his thoughts turn to billiard balls. Nor does he like dogs, for he has *no time for animals, preferring to fawn upon women.* This I hear him say with an expressive pout on his silly lips, lips always a little swollen and moist as though he spent all his time at the breast; lips like the anus of a hen to tell the truth.

"This pampered life will vanish like a dream! Vanish like farts perfumed with anise seeds! Listen to your Fortuné, mistress Josephine! Do not tarry with this tailor's dummy, but follow Boney across the sea! Go be Queen of Egypt! *Wow! Wow! Wow!*"

For my troubles I am thrown from her lap and made to sleep in the hall while her lover reams her with a poker, it is true, of Pharaonic proportions.

How little understood we doggies are!

Because my entreaties failed, I decided to run away. And because we little dogs are susceptible to love too, I attempted to entice Madame Menfous's lapdog Mina to run away with me.

"Do you know," I began, "that our breed goes back to the times of the Romans? Lapdogs slept at Caesar's feet and Pharaoh's too! Already five thousand years ago, house dogs, turnspits, and spaniels sweetened the hours of warrior lords and kings! Did you know that there are no less than one hundred and eighty-five varieties of domestic dogs alone? What I am attempting to convey to Your Sleepiness," I said, not without irritation, "is that we are not *ornaments* but members of an ancient and noble race. That rather than grow old gnawing on slippers, my Mina could be gamboling on the plains of Giza beneath the Pyramids!"

"If you want to see a pyramid so badly," she sighed, "grab your leash and trot over to the Parc Monceau."

"Bah!" I barked, wounded to the quick. "A mere *Turquerie!*"

She was hopelessly Old Regime, perfumed, a pearl stud in her ear, her tail festooned with ribbons. As I spoke her eyelids grew heavier and heavier.

"How hard it is to dream here!" I blurted out, feeling sadder than I'd ever felt. "I am so alone!" I sobbed. *"Wow! Wow! Wow!"*

"There is nothing worse," Mina drawled dismally, before easing herself into a commodious slumber, "than a little black dog who feels sorry for himself."

So there I was, left to chase chimeras alone with no hope for a cure. To keep myself from sinking into desolation, I planned my escape once we hit Toulon. From there Boney's ship, *l'Orient* (*l'Orient! Wow! Wow!*), was to depart for the Mediterranean, and I intended to slip aboard unnoticed—which would be a piece of cake, such was the excitement. The scholars were reading Herodotus aloud to one another and the *Arabian Nights;* the artists were sharpening their pencils and visibly salivating over the prospect of drawing turbaned Turks, Mamelukes, and palm-leaf capitols! *Wow! Wow!* Discomfited by that ignoble device, the leash, I dragged my mistress into the fray. There was Vivant Denon looking for all the world like a Labrador retriever, and Prosper Jollois like a fox terrier. Edme François Jomard had something of the borzoi to command him, and André Dutertre the Great Dane. What a fine crew of cognizant mammals they made! All yipping and yapping together! *Wow! Wow!*

But my project was foiled: in order to disentangle herself from Boney with grace, my mistress promised to join him in Alexandria once the French position was secured. Fools that we were, Boney and I both believed her. I sat in her arms quietly as the *l'Orient* set sail, thinking: The next time that will be me on my way to Egypt!

Later in Paris, I listened for all I was worth whenever conversation turned to the Campaign. In this way I learned of the Mamelukes' defeat, how with swords raised they charged across the desert on horses laden with portable treasures: pocket-sized Korans bound with gold, poison rings studded with coral. Despite their finery, their faith and ferocity, and to their own amazement, they were mowed down by cannonballs and musket fire, their yellow turbans rolling like pumpkins across the sands and also their heads. Bleeding in silk brocade the survivors of the first sally threw themselves by the thousands into the Nile, where they were swept away looking in death like rare flowers blooming on the surface of the waters, their lustrous faces stilled forever, their jeweled vests sparkling in the sun, their purses of gold spilling open, the jaws of eager crocodiles waiting downriver and, thrashing in the sands, their abandoned and wounded horses screaming till dusk! *Wow! Wow!* "Those poor horses!" I sobbed. "Mina! Screaming till dusk! The sand purple with blood!" But she would not quicken to these tales. Instead of inspiring her, they, to use her phrase, *made her uncomfortable.*

"Why can't you settle down," she complained, "and accept that you are a little dog like any other? Let's grow old quietly together, taking pleasure in our daily pâté and cozy quarters, at peace with the world the way it is and with one another."

It was too late. I was no longer a mere biological being but one capable of reverie which—or so it came to me— free of the encumbrances of alphabets, soars to metaphysical goals. I had to accept that with such a frivolous creature as Mina, bred to be a plaything, an exalted love, a brilliant career, were impossible. After that horrible conversation, when I realized that all that was noble in me, imaginative and profoundly alive *frightened her,* I began to disintegrate. A tender, fastidious dog, I grew irritable. And how does a little dog ease his pain? Our sign of discontent is vomit and excrement; these I left liberally in the center of my mistress's bed.

My veritable destiny, I thought to myself when having scolded me Josephine locked me in the scullery, my veritable destiny was to be the dog of a Natural Historian or, better still, an archaeologist, or even the mascot of a general like Boney. To be the dog of a searcher, a dreamer's dog, and yes! *Wow! Wow!* A *dreamy* dog and an intrepid traveler. How eagerly would I plunge my quivering nostrils into the fragrant lilies of the Nile or inquire into rubble after winged scarabs and the mummies of cats. How eagerly would I leave these dreams behind to embrace the adventure both Mina and Josephine call *ridiculous.*

I was dying of longing.

"You were twitching in your sleep." Mina leapt down

from Madame Menfous's lap and prodded me with her paw. "There is nothing more ludicrous than a little black dog dreaming. Besides, why would you want to go to Egypt? The country swarms with crocodiles that, when they get the chance, snap up pugs like sausages."

"I would far rather finish in the gullet of a crocodile," I cried, "than die of boredom beside a bolster in a Parisian boudoir."

"You are no better than mad!" she cried, sticking out a tongue the color of raw salmon. Its color conjured her unspeakably delicate *trou de cul*. I was at a loss for words but could only gaze at her with thwarted affection.

"I am *not* mad!" I said at last, wanting to convey a virile conviction but instead sounding childish and petulant. "I am not mad," I said again, softly, "not mad, little Mina, but only tired to death of this mediocre life. I cannot help but think of the conversations we could be privy to in Cairo at this instant. Or wonder what the world looks like from atop Pompey's Pillar! I cannot help but imagine you, Mina, napping beside the temple of Edfu, your fur gleaming red in the sun of late afternoon. Don't you see? While they are making history—more than that! While they are resurrecting an entire universe, you and I are here snoozing to the redundancies of birdbrained and swiftly aging beauties who spend their lives comparing the qualities of laxatives, powders, and rouge!"

"You are hard on my sex," Mina sniffed. Turning away, her little tail raised like a flag over her unforgettable, eternally blushing *trou de cul,* she leapt back upon Madame Menfous's lap.

Poor, frivolous creature! I thought. But, at least she is mine. Well . . . *almost.* I was foolish enough, you see, to with complacency assure myself that this was so. For, who else could there be? The only other dog not neutered in the vicinity was Creon, the cook's bull mastiff, whose idea of a good time was snapping the spines of cellar rats. How wrong I was, though, not to consider him!

"What I envy of human creatures the most," I said to Mina one day, attempting once again to ignite a flame, no matter how fleeting, "is their sense of history, which is also a sense of selfhood. We dogs live from day to day concerned only with what shows up in our little dish, the bush where we leave our impoverished hieroglyph to be read by a rival or an admirer we may meet, perhaps, for an instant in the street—one who, like ourselves, is straining, *straining* at the leash.

"In my better moments I am grateful for this history-lessness, for I feel timeless and weightless, somehow eternal, like a conscious spark of light. In such moments I forget my name: *Fortuné.* And I forget my color and size. I forget, even, that I am a dog! At such moments I am only a spark shining between two brackets of darkest night. A brief shining to be sure! And yet, and yet . . . I know this instant of burning peace is shared by all dogs—even you,

Mina! Yes! That knowledge of the ineffable. That constancy of light!"

"Oh shut up!" Mina put her paws over her ears. "How you yammer on!"

"Douce amie," I whispered, more to myself than to her, whispered words Boney had once written to my mistress in a letter, "if only you would let me I would ignite you with a kiss." But Mina had heard and showing her teeth she snarled.

"It is time I left," Madame Menfous said to my mistress as she slipped Mina into her basket. "See how ill-tempered Poops is today!"

"Poops!" I snarled back at her, my illusions shattered at last. For one fulgent instant I saw her for what she was: a dim-witted, mean-spirited dachshund, bowlegged and with a waddle. My cosmical gestures would have been comical had they not been tragic.

A day passed and another. Soon I, in my loneliness, began once more to dream of her, to dream of my Mina. With every passing hour I missed her more. Mina! So still, so soft, so pretty! I missed her nose like licorice and yes, even her airs, her frivolity, the way she would snap at flies in her sleep.

And then one afternoon when I least expected it, there she was! Looking like silk, smelling like clover—for she had been rolling in the grass of the Bois de Boulogne. I sat

at the open window admiring her as she crossed the courtyard frisking beside her mistress's shoes.

Then, to my horror, I saw Creon leap from the kitchen
and bound across the cobbles. *Wow! Wow!* I warned Mina
from my window: *Wow! Wow!* Look out! Creon will snap
you in two! But no, instead the brute was bowing before
her, stretching out his paws only to leap up wagging and
prancing in all his oversized earnestness, robust, as speckled
as a quince and muscular—it is true—to court my Mina! I
saw Mina, her bottom oscillating, her ribbons flashing;
Mina so alive, so irreplaceable, so unattainable—gaze at
him and smile. And then before I could turn away it happened: the brute's nose was plumb beneath her tail and she
was not complaining but instead standing still as a piece of
crockery. The pain I felt at that moment was such I feared
it would strike me down. I hoped it would!

Cruel friend, Boney had written to my mistress. *Cruel
friend who loves another!* And there it was! Mina, too, loved
another. Around and around the two dogs went, relishing
those first instants of erotic recognition as our mistresses
made merry with the cook. It was too much. All the disap-
pointments of the past months submerged me in a Nile's
worth of despair. It was as though the deepest dreams and
longings of my soul were revealed to me as mere illusions,
tricks of sunlight in the dust of the air. The glimmer of
eternity of which I'd spoken to Mina was extinguished and
a shadow had descended upon the beauty of the world. I
saw my future: a little dog on a leash forever, a pretentious

pug longing for the impossible. And this longing was a trap, the gilded bone of self-deception.

My sight grew troubled and dim. How could I live without love? Without hope? Without longing? How could I live without ardor? Without a crumb of grandeur? How could I continue living indecorous days gnawing on scraps and inwardly gazing? My dream was irreclaimable. I was deaf to the infinite languages of the world: the wind, the bees, the whispered words of leaves—Isis, Isis, Isis—; the books I could not read but only imagine, the voyages I could not take but only hunger for, the Egypt *Wow! Wow!* I could never see.

Despite the window's height I leapt into the courtyard and fatally, with the cry of a desperate heart, leapt barking at Creon, leapt into those terrible jaws that yawned with the promise of inevitable crime. Josephine screamed and even Mina, Mina! piteously whined.

I have found the promise of the world, I thought as Creon seized me by the neck and with fury shook me. *And now I have lost it.*

Opium

Once, not long ago, the Pope issued a bull extending his powers across all territories known and unknown, illusive yet looming, dreamed and undreamed; and to all crimes against the Church, known and unobserved, ancient and newly rehearsed.

But now this Pope of infinite powers, who has the authority to transform living souls into torches, and who—in the simplest things—has discerned a sorcerous complexity, is himself failing. In a dream he imagines that he is a lump of hot and heavy matter slowly receding, as if time were a silent vortex and his fall both final and without risk. Cushioned by opium, his fall is delicious. Steadily he sinks into his feather bed, almost vanishing altogether much the way the droppings of a polar bear burn their way down through arctic ice before tumbling into an element too deep to be fathomed.

For weeks the Pope's only nourishment has been little balls of opium wrapped in gold leaf and flavored with honey; opium and the milk of a wet nurse. The milk is fed to him from a gold cup. But this morning the Pope makes a request. He wants the wet nurse to come to him herself and suckle him directly. His voice is weak and strange; the words bubble from his tongue like oil from a bottle and yet there can be no doubting his intention: the cup hurts his gums, he has tasted blood, he can no longer lift his head without vertigo. He wants the girl to open her blouse here in his chamber and to cause her breasts to dangle in such a way that he may seize the nipples between his gums.

This is a delicate matter. How may the Grand Penitentiary comply with the hierarch's request without scandal? Hurrying like a huge bird through a succession of apartments, he comes to the door of the chamber where the wet nurse now prepares to ease her milk into the half-moon of glass she holds pressed to a breast. Just as a spray hisses into the glass, the Grand Penitentiary knocks. Startled, the girl and the nun whose special office it is to carry the gold cup to the Pope's chamber, exchange a troubled look. Having announced himself, the Grand Penitentiary steps inside.

The room smells of lactose and of freshly threshed hay; it also smells of verbena: smells that ever after will evoke

the young girl who, her shawl pulled tightly across her
bosom, the glass clasped in her hand, is burning two holes
in the floor with her eyes. The Grand Penitentiary bows
his head and, attempting to put the two women at ease,
aborts a smile. Then fluttering his hands in the air as if to
dispel an invisible threat hovering there, a threat caused by
the sweetness of the girl's own perfume, he bids the nun to
leave. Dissolving, she could not do this more precipitously.

The Grand Penitentiary is standing before the girl, who is
so small he thinks he could crush her with a word. Her
hair is so pale it is almost white and her little hands are no
bigger than a child's. He wonders at her youth; she looks
no more than twelve. Why is she not a virgin spinning in
her father's house? As she stands before him trembling, he
recognizes that the situation makes him anxious also. And
floods him with shame. The milk, until this moment an
abstraction, is, he sees this now, a sexual fluid. He wonders
if there is an infant at home. Or if the infant, her first, for
whom the milk was intended, is dead.

"Child in Christ," he manages at last. To his terror and
surprise she lifts her gaze from the floor and with two
perfectly clear, gray eyes, eyes spinning like the wheels of
perdition, needles him through and through. He turns
away and utters a prayer; recalls how in the presence of the
sumptuous courtesan sent to seduce him in his cell, Blessed

Thomas took up a branch from the hearth and putting it to his loins, quenched his own fire.

"The Pope . . . ," he says. "The Pope . . ."

✍

The morning they found her, a mole had made its way into the kitchen so that when she was asked to follow the Papal messenger, she was amazed that such unprecedented good fortune should attend a bad omen. But now when she hears the Pope's request she knows she is doomed. As she follows the Grand Penitentiary down the hall and into deep rooms thick with tapestries and gilded stoves, she falters and her shawl slips to the floor. She treads upon it, and the half-moon of glass she has held so tightly slips from her fingers and breaks in two. As from out of the air a page smelling of amber appears. Picking up the pieces he vanishes.

"No matter," the Grand Penitentiary whispers as he cleanses the air with his fingers. "It doesn't matter."

✍

Although the day has only just dawned and a gray light soaks the city, entering the Pope's bedchamber is like entering a cathedral at midnight. All the curtains have been pulled and the room's bilious atmosphere is blistering with more candles than she has ever seen. These candles illume the figures of angels that in the flickering light appear to scurry up and down the walls like monkeys among the tendrils and vines of an enchanted forest. Or troops of evil angels riding saddled owls and even the old gods, cloven-hooved and horned: the figures evil women use to inflame the passions of their rival's husbands and kill infants in the crib. These figures adorn cabinets and candlesticks, chairs and chests and the Pope's own bed, and are reflected in and multiplied by mirrors. The walls of the Papal chamber are crusted with mirrors: should the Evil One ever manage to enter here, he will be struck down by the compounded shock of his own fatal glance. But the wet nurse thinks the mirrors do not exorcise evil so much as conjure it. She has heard of the nocturnal orgies of witches and imagines they take place in rooms such as this.

So great is the girl's astonishment, so great her terror, that upon entering the Pope's chamber she neglects to make the sign of the cross. To bring her to her senses, the Grand Penitentiary pinches her arm.

"*Fe* and *Minus*," he murmurs, thinking: The feminine is far too feeble to persist in the Faith. Still pinching the flesh of her arm he leads her to the Pope's bed, recalling the previous day, when a girl not much older than this one had been chained to an iron ring. The ring was attached to an iron pole set in a circle of fire. From a Vatican window he had watched as the girl ran around and around in her attempt to escape the fire. He imagines the wet nurse running within a circle of fire.

✐

A tasseled canopy yawns over the Pope's bony head like a mouthful of gold teeth. She sees the stubborn beak of his nose, his hands like talons gripping an ivory crucifix the size of a small tree. As she unties her blouse, he opens his eyes. Those eyes are blind and this is a consolation. When she bends over the bed, her breast tumbles forth, shining like a planet in the firelight. The Grand Penitentiary reminds himself that if her breast, her throat and lips are smoother than oil, her womb is as bitter as wormwood.

There is so much smoke in the room that when the Pope gums her nipple she coughs. Her nipple leaps from the Pope's mouth making a sound which evokes childish laughter. Peering about her as best she can she sees a tiny black child dressed in white lace and circumventing the room with an aspergillum and holy water. She has never before seen a black child and she is astonished to see one here in the dying Pope's chamber. Was he a gift or had he been purchased? This power of the rich to buy the bodies and lives of others causes her to weep. Studded with pearls, the Pope's nightcap soaks up her tears.

✐

She returns to the Pope's chamber in the afternoon. Entering the room she looks up into the Grand Penitentiary's eyes, which reflect the candle flames and glitter as though made of glass. Because she is wildly superstitious, when she sees those flames in those eyes she fears for her soul. And he, looking into her eyes in turn, sees a little man. Once again he knows he must guard himself against her.

The Pope drinks from her body without eagerness. She thinks that her life is seeping into a dark place like a dark hole of soft earth and wonders at the world's strangeness. Why has God caused her own little one to die that she may give suck to a moribund? For some reason she recalls how her brooding turtledove seemed to sob just as her hatchlings broke free from their shells. Moving near, the little African in his astonishing white dress offers her a shy smile. She wonders what would happen to her if she ran from the room with him. And in the village—what would they say if she took him for her own? What would the child say when she fed him barley gruel and black bread? She supposes his enslavement is sweetened with spice cake and jam—things she has never herself tasted.

When having once more circled the room he approaches her again, she asks him what he is given to eat, and is it served on a gold plate? But the Grand Penitentiary is beside her and with a grimace silences her, although this afternoon the room is sighing with a conclave of cardinals; they rustle in their red robes like wind in sails; they whisper unceasingly to one another.

The following morning when she offers her breast, the Pope does not drink. Instead when he opens his mouth, a gold ball falls out and catches to the lace of his pillow. This astonishes her and she stares at the thing in awe. Later in the day the Pope dies, and as the air shudders with the

tolling of bells she is taken to an inner courtyard paved
with stones as white and round as ostrich eggs, and there
her neck is broken.

Not long after, the new Pope issues a bull dividing all the
world's undiscovered places between the Spanish and the
Portuguese. A vast number of ships set sail for Africa and
India although those lands swarm with infidels, astrologers,
druggists, alchemists, and planetarians. It is easy to find
men eager to join in the adventure of territorial expansion,
for all Europe stinks of burning flesh. The promise of sea
air, of breaking heads with mattocks and axes, of pillaging
flourishing cities, of poisoning fountains of sweet water
with the corpses of camels and children; to in the name of
the Holy See cut off so many noses and ears the land of
Ormuz will appear to be populated by lepers; to destroy all
those who worship the sun, the moon, the lamp, and
cows, and those who hold trees sacred, and those who
worship the circumpolar stars which never set, and those
who worship the whirlwind, the hurricane, and waves on
water; to annihilate the princes of Malabar who feed the
crows before feeding themselves; to slay men who for
medicine inhale the powdered dung of leopards and drink
the urine of virgins—inspires several generations of men.
Restless at sea they dream of the four tastes of the oranges
of Celam, of certain hairy caps from the Levant and weap-
ons made by wizards; of gold plugs taken from the ears of

kings and red and white coral shaped and strung; of pieces of true musk the size of a fist and loaves of coarse camphor; of fine rose water kept in little barrels of tinned copper, of earth from the tomb of Saint Thomas and of opium from Aden. Upon returning they will bring a white elephant to kneel at the feet of the Pope and they will scatter the gems made by Adam's tears across the Pope's path.

For these acts of war, of faith and of longing, they will be awarded miracles: phantom earthquakes, the sight of a mosque spontaneously combusting, of a Moorish king struck down by lightning, the vision of a white city filled with cries but devoid of inhabitants. And they will be awarded glory, which, like riches and miracles—or so they imagine—buys sufficient time to aspire to immortality.

The Word "Desire"

for Jonathan

S he awakens late, their limbs in disorder, his heart quick against her ribs. She feels his cock stir against her thigh. She imagines it has a life of its own because although he appears to be fast asleep, his cock is wide awake, *its own animal* she thinks, thick and hard and thrashing. He sighs, opens his eyes, laughs softly, and with his body covers her. Taking her wrists in his hands he enters her.

She is still wet from the last time—when was it? *Once, twice,* in the middle of the night. They are new lovers—or so it seems; they have been lovers for two years now, perhaps longer. It has always been impossible for her to keep track of the time, to recall when things have taken place, even important things. She cannot remember when it was that he took her for the first time, but will never forget that wealth of dark delight. *Unlike anything else.* He is saying it now: *unlike anything ever known before.* A lucent event like a trespass within a sacred space. When he fucks her, as he is fucking her now, she loses specificity; she crosses over the threshold from solid to fluid, steps into a tender vortex, into a moon-drenched sea, a sun-drenched country.

∞

Now they are on the highway heading west. The landscape opens before them like a body: it spreads and heaves. And they, they are at the heart of the world; they are in its hand and at the center of its eye. They *are* the eye of the world: at their retina's surface the desert burns. She is luxuriating, gazing out, thinking how the word "desire" illuminates their lives; how far the word "desire" has taken them. From time to time she moves her face against his arm, or takes his hand to her lips to gently bite his fingers, suck his fingers, causing him to laugh, to reach over and put his hand between her legs, to, with intimacy, explore her. For a moment the sun ignites the car. She thinks how before electricity the sun was a great power, was *the* great power. She thinks how the world oscillates about this power. An interminable event of seduction. She thinks: *Gravity is a species of fascination.*

∞

Now they see the ruins rising along the rim of the sky, espousing the cliffs—a natural fortress—all openings facing outward. They have left behind rubble and scree, low-growing sage, scrub oak, and are entering a woodland. For a few moments the ruins and the cliff are concealed. Just before they pull into the parking lot, a jeweled lizard runs across the road on its hind legs, runs with the vibrancy and purpose of a sacred thing, before vanishing.

They begin their climb. The paths are narrow, cut into stone. The ancient city rises above them like many faces, numberless eyes and mouths open for speaking. The city is as simple as the bones of an animal and it is painful to imagine the landscape without it: it is like imagining an animal without its spine. They continue to climb, and soon the city dissolves beneath them. They have reached a sacred place, a bowl-shaped platform seemingly suspended in the air and reflecting the sun like a mirror of polished metal. As the sun spills down the flanks of the mountain opposite, dazzling her where she stands, she is seized by the primacy of the moment and she imagines all those who have stood as she stands, illumed and warmed by the sun. She imagines all those who will come after, virtual strangers like blossoms threaded by time into garlands. Wanting to say: *I feel so alive!* She turns to him.

But he is not looking to the mountains; he does not see the sun spilling into the valley. Instead he is gazing with intensity toward the path. There is heat in his eyes, a fire she knows well: it is the fire of their first encounter, a look of dark avowal; his gaze is directed like an arrow of fire across the way to a woman who is standing alone gazing—

as she has been gazing—to the west. The woman is beautiful—*his type* she thinks, *dark, like me.* The woman stands
still, so still beneath his gaze in that sacred theater, that it is
clear to her the woman knows she is being watched. *Who
is the trespasser here? How can this be?* How can this be that
he stands on his own piece of turf as it were, stands apart
from her, out of her orbit, so distant as though nothing
joined them? Had ever joined them? Not a thread of saliva,
nor an amorous word.

Now the air is very thin. Her bones too, are thin, and
her skin (above all her skin!) so thin it no longer keeps her
warm. For a moment she longs to dissolve, to vanish, to
vanish into the other woman. To be the other woman; to
lift her eyes and take in his gaze for the first time. To
receive his gaze as a landscape is flooded with sunlight.

A curious inversion takes hold. As she looks at him
gazing at the other woman, she is no longer looking at
him, but looking from within him. She has become his
eyes, so to speak. The immeasurable distance she had
imagined between them has vanished. And this bewitching
inversion does not stop there because suddenly she *is* the
other woman, aware that he is gazing at her. He, a stranger
now, is seizing her with his eyes, entering her with his
gaze, possessing her. His eyes are like daggers of light, as
though fucking were an attribute of light, as though looking were consuming, and the retina a place of burning.

Because she is an artist, she knows the eye hungers. At
that moment it is revealed to her that her lover is seeing

with his sexual soul, that his eyes are revealing this most compassionate place within himself. She knows this place intimately and yet as often as she has entered there, has been irresistibly drawn there, still it remains a power and a mystery. Gazing through his eyes at the other, receiving her lover's heat through the other's body, it is revealed to her that she is not dreaming nor inventing this, but that she is witness to a simple and essential experience of seeing. And being.

An instant later, vertigo overtakes her. She thinks: *But what will happen?* And she catches her breath. He turns to her then and says: *Shall we go?* She cannot meet his eyes now—her own eyes are so thin with seeing they are a fragile paper. Should he look into them, they will tear. As though glued to the spot, looking into the sun, she nods. He says: *It is beautiful.* She wonders: *What is he naming beautiful? And who?*

The other has turned away; she has begun to move gracefully—an agile female animal—down the path. She admires the woman's animal movements. Something about the way she moves reveals that she knows he is still watching her and *it is true,* she thinks, *her form is lovely, her gaze bewitching; has he tired of me so quickly? What will happen? And what is this power that opens and shuts within me like the eye of a camera? And who are the trespassers here? And who are the seekers?* She knows the answer: They are all seekers. She thinks: *How far the word "desire" goes! How it tugs us along! How it worries us, daggers us! How it lights our path.*

They descend into trees and the path becomes many paths. Theirs heads east and now they are alone. Like a light gone out, like an extinguished flame, the other woman is gone without a trace. She feels this. In her bones and blood she feels this: the other has left no trace. She feels his heat, his substantiality, his intelligence receiving the world. Even before he reaches out to put his hand gently at the back of her neck she quickens; her skin fits over her muscles and bones exactly.

Ever after, each time he embraces her, the other woman and her vanishment informs her passion—not because the fear of his loss excites her lust, but because the other woman revealed this: Desire is a figment swiftly fleeting, an ephemeral enactment upon the finite stage of the mutable world, and flesh a flame and a seeming. *Is it true then,* she thinks, *all is fire?* This knowledge, given her by her rival, her sister, the stranger, fans the pleasure she shares with him, instants of delight dissolving as they happen, collapsing into themselves just as time collapses into itself, and as the two of them collapse into one another after love.

You see: it was as if that afternoon she had stepped over a threshold. Thereafter she thinks: *He and I share the same mystery.* Except she believes this: she believes that she is the one who keeps this particular mystery hidden. She believes that he has forgotten the other woman, that the other woman has been replaced over and over again by other chance encounters, other faces igniting the world like suns. And she believes that each time he embraces her, her own body eclipses the others, or—better still—*exemplifies* the others. So that her intimate life with him is a fusion of memory and desire and will: the will to be unique, to be uniquely his, to live each unique instant fully—and the will to *be* desire, to be the infinite faces of desire; to be one word and that word is ''desire.''

Now she has, at least to herself, confessed everything. There is nothing more to confess, except this, and to him: that when she takes his sex into her mouth, between her teeth, against her tongue; when his sex sweetly collides with the back of her throat like a comet hitting the world; when as he enters her face he holds her head between his hands or caresses her hair, her body dissolves into time and she is become an event of lucency. She is become heat and light dissolving between his fingers, the seconds like hot sand spilling through his fingers . . . and then his sperm like a nectar burning in her throat.